Tess turned to him an .n a ges-
ture of 'ssshhh,' as the key once again began to spark and, as
it had the first time, turned to a bright brass color as it neared
the gate. The keyhole appeared out of nowhere. And as the
key connected, the gate, too, transformed as if it were brand
new and totally inviting.

Max broke the silence. "Wow! That was sort of incred-
ible."

Tess stepped in front of Max into the garden. She looked
around to see if William was there. No sign of him. She saw
a lone white dove perched on the branch of a silver birch
tree. And then the yellow ball came whizzing towards her.
She leaned down, without missing a beat, and picked it up
goalie style. She set it down on the ground before her and
folded her arms on her chest.

"Good catch," he shouted to her as she shouted back, almost in unison, "Good shot. But I'm too fast for you."

He walked across the garden to her. "Is it all right," she
asked, "that I brought my brother?"

"Of course it is," he answered.

"William, this is Max. Max, this is William," said Tess,
making a formal introduction between them.

OTHER BOOKS YOU MAY ENJOY

The BFG	Roald Dahl
Carnival Magic	Amy Ephron
The Charmed Children of Rookskill Castle	Janet Fox
Circus Mirandus	Cassie Beasley
A Clatter of Jars	Lisa Graff
Journey's End	Rachel Hawkins
A Little Princess	Frances Hodgson Burnett
Matilda	Roald Dahl
Ms. Rapscott's Girls	Elise Primavera
The Secret Garden	Frances Hodgson Burnett
A Tangle of Knots	Lisa Graff

THE
CASTLE
IN
THE MIST

THE
CASTLE
IN
THE MIST

AMY EPHRON

PUFFIN BOOKS

PUFFIN BOOKS
An imprint of Penguin Random House LLC
375 Hudson Street
New York, New York 10014

First published in the United States of America by Philomel Books,
an imprint of Penguin Random House LLC, 2017
Published by Puffin Books, an imprint of Penguin Random House LLC, 2018

Text copyright © 2017 by Amy Ephron
Map and illustrations copyright © 2017 by Vartan Ter-Avanesyan

THE LIBRARY OF CONGRESS HAS CATALOGED THE PHILOMEL BOOKS EDITION AS FOLLOWS:
Names: Ephron, Amy, author. | Title: The castle in the mist / Amy Ephron.
Description: New York, NY : Philomel Books, [2017] | Summary: "Sent for the summer
to their aunt's sleepy village in the English countryside, Tess and Max find the key to a
castle hidden from time and learn that wishes can come true, if they wish carefully"—
Provided by publisher. | Identifiers: LCCN 2016014561 | ISBN 9780399546983 (hardback)
| Subjects: | CYAC: Castles—Fiction. | Wishes—Fiction. | Magic—Fiction. | Brothers and sisters—Fiction.
| England—Fiction. | BISAC: JUVENILE FICTION / Fantasy & Magic. | JUVENILE FICTION /
Family / Siblings. | JUVENILE FICTION / Social Issues / Friendship.
| Classification: LCC PZ7.1.E62 Cas 2017 | DDC [Fic]—dc23
| LC record available at https://lccn.loc.gov/2016014561

Puffin Books ISBN 9780399547003

Edited by Jill Santopolo. Design by Jennifer Chung.
Text set in 12.25-point Winchester New ITC Std.

Printed in the United States of America

1 3 5 7 9 10 8 6 4 2

For Zachary and Madeline
& their Great Aunt Delia

white horse tavern

antique

Hampshire Rd.

aunt Evie's house

dairy farm

N
W
S
E

THE
CASTLE
IN
THE MIST

CONTENTS

the warning

"Hawthorn trees."

"Please stop saying that."

But Tess said it again, "Haw-thorn trees," emphasizing each syllable.

They were having breakfast at their aunt Evie's house in Hampshire, England, where they were staying for the summer.

"Aunt Evie," said Max, being careful to pronounce

her name properly—*Awnt* the British way, and *Ev-ie*, short for Evelyn, nothing to do with Eve. "Please make her stop, Aunt Evie. She's driving me crazy."

"Hawthorn trees." Tess said it one more time. And then she added, "He told me to be careful of the hawthorn trees."

"I did not," said Max. "I don't even know what a hawthorn tree is."

"Who is the 'he' in that sentence?" asked Evie, suddenly paying attention to Tess.

"A boy I met yesterday—" Tess hesitated since she knew this next part could get her into trouble "—who was walking on the road leading away from town."

"And how old was this boy?"

"Hmm, maybe my age. Or a little older, twelve? I didn't ask. He's very pale and he has a—umm—accent, British sort of, so I'm pretty sure he's from here."

"I don't know an eleven- or twelve-year-old boy who lives around here," Aunt Evie replied. "Maybe he's visiting relatives. Did he say anything else to you?"

Tess thought for a minute. "Umm, no. I mean, he said hello. And then he told me to be careful of the hawthorn trees."

This wasn't exactly true. They'd had a much longer conversation than that, but she didn't know what Aunt Evie would think of the real story . . .

2

the castle in the mist

the real story

She and her brother, Max, had had a fight the day before. Over nothing. It was always over nothing. They were playing Monopoly. The British version, because that was all Evie had in the house besides Scrabble. Tess was winning. Tess had three hotels and she rolled double sixes for the second time in a row, and Max had thrown the board at her. Well, not really at her, but in her direction . . . Tess got mad, too. But rather than having

3

a fight with him, she'd stormed off on her own into the back garden and kept on walking.

Tess never could stay mad at Max for more than half an hour, but it was nice to be outside, the air was fresh, and so she continued walking up the path to where the pear and plum trees were planted on the hill. She stopped and ate a plum and then was surprised to see the path continued beyond the small orchard. She kept on walking, higher and higher. The path stopped at a moment, dead-ended against a hill, but then she took the narrow trail to the right and there was a clear view across a field of tall grass sprinkled with wildflowers. Tess didn't know why she'd never been up here before.

She walked across the small meadow, back onto a path, and up the hill, which was now becoming almost rocky, as if she'd happened onto a cliff. Off to her left, she could see something she'd never seen before; certainly it wasn't visible from the main road, she didn't think. It was an old house, ancient maybe—well, *house* might not be the right word, as it looked awfully large, but it was hard to tell, since it seemed as if it was covered in a cloud of mist.

She stopped on the path, struck by the image of what looked like a castle in the mist, so startling and yet so still, almost as if it was a painting.

There seemed to be steps in the cliff side, carved into the rock, and Tess followed them, slowly. She stopped to look back for a moment. She could see the top of her aunt's house seemingly far in the distance. She realized she might have walked farther than she'd thought. And then the path stopped and there was just the face of a rocky hill above her. She turned to the left and saw a tangled rose bush; its tiny pink flowers reminded her of her mother's garden at their small country house on Long Island.

She sat down on the highest step and looked out over the dark green moors, seemingly endless grass, and what looked like a herd of cows, which must be the dairy farm a half mile down the road from Aunt Evie's. They would go there to get eggs and cream for the week, and fresh butter if he'd made any. They always went to the dairy farm on Mondays. Her aunt said it was a good thing to have a bit of a schedule, especially if you lived alone.

Tess stood up and realized she was a little out of breath from the climb or else she was up so high, the air was thin. She looked again at the tangled rose bush and was surprised to find, just next to it, a wooden gate that was carved. It looked a little like a gingerbread cookie with a funny symbol in the middle, not quite like a heart, more like a coat of arms. The curious thing about the gate, though, was it didn't seem attached to a fence. Tess had noticed that about England—people weren't as big on fences as they were in America; everything wasn't all closed in. She'd asked her aunt about it. Evie had thought it had something to do with old horse trails that linked the neighborhood together and the fact that the houses were so far away from one another. Tess hadn't pressed her on this, but she did wonder if there wasn't a stable nearby and one day her aunt might let them take a riding lesson or at least go out on a ride. Tess loved horses and the way it felt to be up on one. Max wasn't as keen on it, so she hadn't suggested it yet. Still, it was curious that there was a gate and there wasn't any fence. She thought she might as well just walk around it.

She was surprised when she tried. It was as if she'd hit a flat surface. First her toe banged into it and then her shoulder. But there wasn't anything there. Not anything you could see, anyway. She took a step back and put her hand out. It had a smooth surface, cold, almost like polished marble. But there wasn't anything there that she could see and she couldn't quite see through it, either. Like an invisible wall. It was very odd. She walked down to the other side of the gate and tried again. But once again, her toe hit the wall and then she bumped it with her elbow. Something didn't want to let her in. She traced that side with her hand as well, and well, it was curious . . .

She was a little frightened. It didn't make a lot of sense. She wondered if she might have had too much sun and she was imagining things. If she'd had any sense, she probably would've run back down the path to her aunt's house, where everything was just as it was supposed to be.

The gate itself was also odd. It was a carved wooden gate, but it didn't have a latch or a keyhole and its surface was flat, no edges of wood to get a foot on so that you could try to climb over it. It was just high enough so that no amount of jumping could get her to reach the top—not that she was enough of a gymnast to have hoisted herself over, and if she could, she wondered how she would ever get back . . .

She was just about to give up when she looked down and saw a round piece of metal, almost like an iron ring, buried in the dirt. She leaned down and, using her T-shirt like a glove, clawed at the dirt and pulled out what looked like an old skeleton key.

She knew instantly it was the key to the gate. But then she had what her dad would call a dilemma. *If she'd found the key to someone's "house," did it mean she had the right to use it?* Well, it wasn't really the key to the house, she reasoned, it was just the key to the gate. And if there were dogs on the other side, they would've been barking already.

She brushed off the key as best she could, completely forgetting that there wasn't any keyhole to put it in. It was as if she was compelled to try it. She held the key up to the gate and then realized how ridiculous that was, but as the key neared the place where the keyhole should've been, the rust flashed away in an instant—she swore she saw sparks—and the gate seemed to lighten as if it had been built in this century after all. It was almost as if it was a magnet, or two sides of a magnet anyway, as her hand pushed the key into a shiny brass keyhole that appeared out of nowhere. She was a little frightened now, but the gate swung open before she could even turn the key . . .

She could see a pond, the water pale blue, with white swans in it and what seemed like water lilies growing around the banks. There were hedges in the distance, staggered in lines, that reminded her of the maze at Hampton Court. She wondered if it *was* a maze. The hydrangeas were blooming, their lush white flowers looked like pom poms. It was definitely somebody's estate. And now she was worried that the invisible "wall" on either side of the gate was like an electrified fence or something—her father had told her about those—and she really shouldn't be there at all.

But before she could shut the gate and run back down the hill, a voice called out, "Hello-o." There was a boy who looked to be almost her age kicking a yellow ball, practicing soccer moves. He stopped the ball adeptly between his feet and called out again, "Hello." And then he added the strangest thing, "I've been expecting you."

Tess put her hand on her hip and said, "Really? What's my name, then?"

The boy stammered, "I didn't mean, I didn't, I meant I'd been expecting someone." And then he smiled and added, "But I'm awfully glad it's you." Leaving the ball on the grass, he started to walk towards her. "I'm William," he said. "What's your name?"

"Tess," she answered. "Tess Barnes." Something made her want to tell him her last name, too. There was something about the house that made her want to seem proper. She wondered if he was a Prince or his father was a Lord or something. The property was awfully grand.

"I didn't mean to burst in," she said.

He laughed at that. "You hardly burst in. You were just standing at the gate."

Tess turned back to look at the gate, which was still

ajar. She turned back to ask him about it, but before she could, he said, "It's better that we not speak about that. Take the key. Don't shut the gate. Take the key out of the lock and put it in your pocket. That way you can come back and visit me again, if you want."

There was something about the way he said it, quickly and as if it was an instruction, that made her wonder what would happen if she didn't take the key out of the lock. If the gate could close and neither one of them would be able to get out. She was letting her imagination run away with her. Not really, the whole thing had been a little strange.

She quickly put her hand on the gate though and pulled the key out from the lock. In an instant the keyhole disappeared. The key, though, was still the bright brass color it had turned when she'd put it in the lock.

"You don't need it?" Tess asked.

"No, it doesn't work from this side." He saw her looking at the sides of the gate, the invisible wall she had run up against. "It's a trick," he explained. "My father's big on privacy."

Tess sort of understood that. Her father was a little cautious, too. They had emergency kits and all kinds of things stacked up in a closet. There were flashlights in almost every drawer, not to mention the extra bottles of water and ridiculous amounts of votive candles packed away in the pantry.

"What does he do?" she asked. "Your dad?"

"He's a banker. I think that's what he does. It's sort of complicated, something to do with investing. He spends most of his time in London."

"My dad's a reporter," said Tess. "He's in Afghanistan now."

"Oh," said William, "that's very far away."

Tess laughed. "I guess it is." She was very appreciative that he hadn't said, "Oh, dear," or "That must be dangerous," or given her one of those looks that grown-ups did, as if they were quite concerned, and then they would be extra nice to her.

He told her that Marie, the woman who took care of him, had made him a picnic and he asked if she was hungry. She was, actually. It had been a bit of a hike to get there and she'd stormed out before lunch.

She took a look around the garden. She walked over to the pond and put her hand in the water just to make sure that it was water and not some odd illusion. The flowers smelled the way they were supposed to. And, just there, laid out on the lawn behind where he'd been

11

playing, was a cloth tablecloth and a wicker picnic basket.

"She always makes two kinds," said William. There was ham and cheddar on a kind of brown bread, and cream cheese and strawberry preserves on white bread. The crusts had been cut off and the sandwiches cut into four triangles, very neatly, the same way Aunt Evie cut them. The jam and cream cheese was delicious. She was hungry. The ham was good, too. She could tell it was home-made and not from a package. After they'd finished lunch and folded up the tablecloth, she started to leave. But he kicked the ball to her and, instinctually, she kicked it back.

Tess was good at soccer. It wasn't her favorite sport. But AYSO was all the rage in New York. She had been on one team or another ever since she was five—until two years ago, when she'd finally become more serious about ballet and there was only so much time for extracurricular activities. She hadn't quite lost her touch, though.

"Whoa," he called over his shoulder as he ran after the ball that whizzed right past him, "when you play with two people, it's not supposed to be competitive. It's just supposed to be practice."

She laughed again. She was competitive. She knew that.

"I'll never kick it away from you," he said. "Look behind you."

She wasn't sure what she was supposed to be looking at. Far away, there was a row of tall bushes at the edge of the garden with white flowers that looked wild, as if they'd sort of sprouted like a feather at the top of a leaf, a whole wall of them almost, like a hedge. She looked back at him and he nodded.

"Hawthorn trees," he said.

"Hawthorn trees?"

"Yes, that's what those are." He hesitated. "Stay away from the hawthorn trees," he said.

Before she could ask why, he kicked the ball back to her.

He was awfully good. Sometimes when you play with someone very good, your game gets better. And she began to kick with a kind of aim and determination that she wished she'd used when she was in a league. She could hardly stop herself from playing with him. But it was getting chilly and she could tell the sun had moved considerably in the time that she'd been here.

"I have to get back." It occurred to her that Aunt Evie might be worried. "I didn't realize how late it was." She started to run for the gate. "Thank you for lunch," she called out to him. "It was very nice to meet you."

"Please come back," he called in return as she reached the gate, which was still ajar, and ran out of it. And she heard him say, "Remember—" his voice seemed to echo softly across the moors "—stay away from the hawthorn trees."

She turned back and shut the gate and wasn't at all surprised that, as it closed, it went back to its musty state, like a petrified version of a gingerbread cookie. *Quite a trick,* she thought to herself. And the only possible explanation she could come up with was that it must be like a hologram. That made sense. She looked on both sides of the path, to make sure there weren't any hawthorn trees growing along the side, but it seemed safe.

She ran down the hill so quickly, she stumbled on a step of the rocky cliff. She fell, catching herself with her hands.

She had to stop in the small orchard to take a breath. She was already working out in her head what she would tell her aunt. *She'd gone for a bike ride. It was such a pretty day she kept on riding.* She knew she couldn't tell the real story. Her dad had once told her, "A version of the truth is the best lie." So, she thought she'd just say she'd made a friend. She just didn't think she could explain the whole adventure.

She put her hand in her pocket to find the key. She wasn't at all surprised when she pulled it out that it had gone back to its original rusted state. No, she didn't see any way she could explain this.

the hawthorn trees

I thought I knew everyone around here," said Aunt Evie. "I'm not coming up with an eleven-year-old boy, not from any family I know. They must be summer renters," Aunt Evie declared. "What house did you say he lived in?"

"I don't know where he lives," said Tess. "He was riding a bike, too." That was the ninth lie she'd told in the space of an hour. Or maybe the tenth, as there were two lies in that last bit. She knew exactly where he lived. And he hadn't been riding a bike.

"He told you to be careful of the hawthorn trees," said Aunt Evie, although this sounded more like a question. "I wonder why . . ." She was already out of her chair at the kitchen table and on her way to the parlor. She would return in a moment with *The Big Encyclopedia of Plants and Herbs*. Aunt Evie had a book for everything. If they were home, their mother would have just googled it. On the other hand, if they were home, there would have been wi-fi. This was a particularly sore spot for Max, so Tess didn't mention it.

"Here it is," said Evie, opening the book triumphantly on the kitchen table. There was a black-and-white illustration after the word *hawthorn*, depicting a hedge of trees, tightly knitted together. There were thorns visible on the trunk and delicate flowers on the branches.

Aunt Evie read to herself at first. "Oh, this is interesting," she said aloud. "Hawthorn trees are thought to have medicinal powers and ward off evil spirits. That could be useful. Hmmm." She read a bit more, then said aloud, "In Ireland they believe they're the door to the land of the fairies. Well, we're not in Ireland." Evie read on, speaking a bit as she scanned the rest of the entry.

"They can bring good luck or bad luck . . ." Then her face darkened as if she didn't like the next part she'd read. "This is very complicated," said Aunt Evie, shaking her head at the book as she shut it abruptly. "But I wonder why he told *you* to stay away from them. He sounds like an inciter."

"What's an inciter?" asked Tess.

"Oh, you know, a little boy who likes to make trouble, stir things up, give people the creeps. An inciter can be a grown-up, too."

"He seemed nice actually. I think it was my fault," Tess said quickly. "I got tired and I was walking my bike by the hedge and I think he thought I'd get allergic."

"Are they like poison ivy?" Max asked, already having a vision of pushing his sister into a hawthorn tree the first chance he had. Not that he would do it, but the image was appealing.

"No, the book didn't say anything about that, Max," said Aunt Evie.

"He was very nice, Aunt Evie, and polite." Tess was worried that she'd gotten the boy in trouble and that Evie might not let her play with him again. "He did tell me his name," said Tess, remembering Aunt Evie had a rule that you should always know a person's name if you were speaking to them. "His name is William. He told me his last name," she added, even though this wasn't true at all, "but I can't remember it."

"Well, I wish you knew his last name," said Aunt Evie, "then it would be easier to invite him for tea." She so wanted the children to be happy this summer.

Tess and Max's year had been rocky. Aunt Evie could only imagine. Suddenly last December, they were told abruptly (sort of the way their dad would go off unexpectedly on assignment) that they were going to go to a boarding school in Switzerland.

Switzerland, thought Tess. *What's wrong with Vermont?* But before she could say anything, Max said, "Did we do something wrong?"

"Oh, no, dear," their mom said quickly. Tess couldn't tell for sure but she thought her mom had been crying.

"I think I'll be sent on assignment soon," their dad said. "And, your mom has a book due . . . I have a friend who's the headmaster at the Academy in Montreux, Switzerland, and, well, just think of it as an adventure . . . you know, sort of the way college kids take a year abroad. If I'm in Europe or the Middle East, it'll be easier to visit you on the weekends . . ."

Tess didn't want to tell her dad they were in middle

school, not college. She couldn't tell if this made sense or not, but there was something about the way he said it that made both her and Max realize it was a done deal.

Tess and Max didn't know that their mother was ill . . . She hadn't told anyone but Evie and, of course, their father. Their mother's chances of recovery were good, but the treatment was brutal.

Their dad, Martin Barnes, was a well-known newscaster. He had taken part of the year off to take care of their mom, but now he *was* in Afghanistan. He was a foreign correspondent, which these days mostly meant war reporter. The children's spring term had ended in Switzerland. And their mother still had another month of medical treatments. The whole thing was a mess and there wasn't anyone to send them to but Aunt Evie. It wasn't that she wouldn't have wanted them under normal circumstances, but there wasn't any way to say no under the present ones.

Aunt Evie had looked, but she hadn't been able to find a proper summer camp anywhere in the neighborhood. The only thing she had found was a shooting range. She knew her sister Abby would never forgive her if she sent them off to a rifle range. She could understand why the children might be bored in the country with

one around who was their age except this mysterious William.

"Can I, Aunt Evie, invite him to tea? May I?" Tess corrected herself instantly. "I would like that."

"Of course you can," said Aunt Evie, "and you may. But I wonder why he told you to stay away from the hawthorn trees."

"I wonder that, too," said Tess.

Tess also wondered if she would be brave enough to try to find him again . . .

the curious antique store

It was Sunday, so they would go into town to The White Horse Tavern for dinner, which was on North Hampton Road. Every other day, The White Horse Tavern was off-limits to Tess and Max. The patrons had to be over 21, which their aunt said was a good thing, as it could get a little rowdy in there—except on Sunday nights, when they served dinner or, as their aunt called it, Sunday Supper.

Aunt Evie had an old Bentley that she took very good care of. It had leather seats that were soft and almost the color of caramel. Aunt Evie told Tess that it had been Uncle John's car and that she was going to keep it always. Tess was pretty sure she would. Evie and Uncle John had had what their mom referred to as "a true" love. And when Uncle John died so unexpectedly in a skiing accident two years before, it had quite startled everyone. Aunt Evie was only 38, young to be a widow. She immediately sold the flat in London and moved to the house in Hampshire, which had been John's family's home. Her sister, Abby, worried that Evie would be lonely and isolated there. But Evie insisted she had friends in the country and that it was the place that reminded her of John the most. She said that was what she wanted for now. But Aunt Evie also had to admit that she liked having her niece and nephew there. She liked the sound of them laughing upstairs. She *had* been spending too much time on her own. She liked going out with them for Sunday Supper.

The Bentley was always well polished. It was navy-blue and very big inside. Evie wore a red scarf around her neck and leather driving gloves and, if the weather was nice, put her hair up in a ponytail and put the top down.

Tess thought Aunt Evie looked like a movie star when she drove it. Tess always sat in the back because Max got carsick, although Tess didn't think he'd dare get sick in Aunt Evie's Bentley. Tess liked to tilt her nose up in the air and pretend that there was a glass divider between her and the front seat (like a car she'd been in once with her father) and that she was really a princess.

But on this particular Sunday night, the twilight hour was sparkly, still light, the dew on the grass seemed to shine with color, the cows dotting the nearby field looked like a picture, and strangely menacing—something Tess had never noticed before—a thick row of hawthorn trees, their white flowers waving like feathers, just before they reached the town. *Note to self: be sure to ride your bicycle on the right side of the road on the way to town.* That was something her mother always said: Note to self. But her mother kept a notebook with her and actually jotted it down. Tess just did it in her head.

"Aunt Evie," Tess shouted from the back seat, "look, the antique store's open." They were about to drive right past it. Evie had mentioned to Tess that she'd broken an antique wine glass and wanted to try to replace it the next time they passed an antique store.

Aunt Evie turned the Bentley sharply into the driveway,

almost without slowing down, kicking up a lot of dirt in the parking lot as she pulled to a stop just at the side of the shop.

"Thanks for remembering," Aunt Evie said. "Let's see if they have anything like it. It's just the sort of thing it's impossible to match."

The bells on the shop door jingled slightly when they entered, but there was no one in the front of the store. There were hardly any lights on and the place was eerily quiet. "Why don't we just look around," said Aunt Evie, "and I'm sure someone will come up soon."

Max found a box of old postcards and sat down on the floor to look at them. Aunt Evie went to examine the china closets. Tess wandered off on her own, past glass display cases filled with jewelry, to the back of the store and found a wooden table with sign that said: SALE 50% OFF. She studied the items on the table. Tess thought she might find a present for her mom. There was a silver bracelet with purple stones, but it looked like it might be too small for her mother's wrist, and possibly too expensive. There was a carved elephant with an upturned trunk that had a little attitude but seemed too delicate for shipping. And then, Tess's eye was caught by something at the very back edge of the table. Two candlesticks, blackened from age, so she couldn't tell if they were bronze or silver, very simply designed, almost straight up and down with a little square plate just where the candle would set in, a thin stem, and a similar square base. And, Tess noticed, just below the square where the candle would go was the same image that she'd seen the day before, the same symbol that was etched into the skeleton key and carved in the wooden gingerbread-like gate that opened to the garden of the castle in the mist. She carefully picked the candlesticks up off the table and brought them to the front of the store.

The shopgirl, a pixie-like thing with red hair that was so curly it stood out on its own, had appeared and was standing behind the front counter. Tess set the candlesticks down.

The shopgirl had a strong accent. "My mum," the girl said, "when my mum put those out on the table this morning, she said that she was sure someone was going to come for them today. And here y'are."

Tess couldn't tell if she was reading something more into this statement than she should have been—if it was just a cunning shopgirl trying to make a sale—but she felt a small shiver when the girl said it.

"I thought they might be a good present for my mom," Tess said. "Do you think she'd like them?"

"Probably," said Aunt Evie. "Your mom likes simple things."

And, Tess thought to herself, *they have the same mark on them as the gate and the skeleton key . . . whatever that might mean . . .* For a moment, Tess thought she saw them sparkle, a bright golden light, right at the place where the symbol was. *No, it must've been a reflection from the lights on the ceiling.*

"I have money at home, Aunt Evie . . ." Tess said.

"That's okay, Tess. I think I can spring for them for you and your mom. I didn't find a wine glass, anyway."

"Didn't you?" the girl asked. "I thought that was y'rs."

Aunt Evie looked at the counter, and right next to the candlesticks was an antique crystal wine glass.

"That's curious," said Aunt Evie. "It's identical to the ones I have at home, I think, but I didn't put it there . . ." Aunt Evie looked at the price tag and instantly said, "That's a deal."

"Well, I guess that was meant to be, then, too," the young woman said. And then she added, almost as if she were talking to herself, "Sometimes things really are just meant t' be."

Aunt Evie also bought Max five antique marbles that were pretty and, the shopgirl insisted, hand-blown glass.

The girl threw in two long, fresh wax candles as a gift. "My mum makes these," she said as she wrapped them and the candlesticks in brown paper, carefully wrapped the wine glass in tissue, put it in its own bag, and put Max's marbles in another, smaller brown paper bag.

Aunt Evie paid and the three of them left the antique store. Tess heard the shop bells jingle again slightly as the shop door closed. It was just beginning to rain.

"Curious," said Aunt Evie as they all bundled back into the Bentley and headed toward The White Horse Tavern for dinner, "I don't think I've ever seen that shop open before."

Somehow, Tess was starting to think, *that might not be curious, at all.*

They settled into the red booth in the back of the dining room after Aunt Evie said hello to practically everyone in the restaurant. The back booth was officially Aunt Evie's table on Sunday nights and it had a sign on it that said RESERVED.

They ordered the prime rib dinner. They always ordered the prime rib dinner. She and Max split one because it was enormous. Even the baked potato, filled with butter and sour cream and chives, could be split in half and neither of them could even finish it. There was Yorkshire pudding. Tess always asked for honey to drizzle on it. Even the spinach was good. *Note to self: ask Aunt Evie to ask Mrs. McEvoy for her creamed spinach recipe.*

Tess had a notebook, too, that she wrote in sometimes. She kept it under her mattress. She didn't want anyone to read what she said. It was sort of a diary, but sometimes she wrote poems, too. She knew Max would make fun of her if he found it. She decided she would not write about her adventure in her notebook. She also decided that she would write her mother a letter and tell her that she'd made a friend. She would leave out a lot of detail, but there were some secrets that it was fun to share—like the fact that she'd made a friend. She did wonder when the next time was that she would be able to go and visit him . . .

● ● ●

Tess fell asleep in the car on the way back to Aunt Evie's.

Half awake, she barely made it up the stairs and into her pajamas.

As her head hit the pillow, she remembered the key. She'd thrown her shorts on the blue-and-white striped velvet chair by the dresser.

Please let it be there. Please let it be there. She said silently to herself, wondering how she could have been so careless. It was. The rusty old skeleton key was right in her pocket where she'd left it. She got an envelope from her stationery box, dropped the key in, and sealed the envelope. She wrote the words *The Castle in the Mist* on it in her best cursive, which would turn out to be one of the stupider things she'd done in the last six months. She hid it in her sweater drawer, the third one down in the dresser, underneath a pale beige button-down sweater her mother had given her for her last birthday.

She got back into bed, turned the bedside light off again, and within moments fell fast asleep. Not surprisingly, she dreamt about swans.

keeping secrets

It was after ten when Tess went down for breakfast. One of the nice things about Aunt Evie was that she didn't believe in schedules. Evie thought it was perfectly okay to stay up all night reading, particularly if the book was good. The only thing she insisted on was that they all have dinner together.

Every morning, Aunt Evie made oatmeal, which she left on in the slow cooker for Max and Tess. The truth is,

Tess was getting a little sick of oatmeal, but this morning it had apples and raisins in it, even though it had sat for so long, it was sort of the consistency of mashed potatoes. It was a little chilly still in the kitchen, so Tess ran upstairs to get a sweater.

When she opened her bedroom door, there was Max holding an envelope, staring at it curiously. She realized in an instant it was the envelope she'd written on so foolishly last night.

"You know you're not supposed to go through my things," Tess yelled at him.

"I wasn't going through your things! Aunt Evie always mixes up our laundry. I was looking for my blue jacket."

"You're supposed to ask me before you do that! Give it to me!" She grabbed for the envelope.

Max smiled his most impish smile and held the envelope up above his head. Tess was relieved to see he hadn't opened it. It was sort of laughable that he was holding it over his head because she was just as tall as he was, actually an inch taller. She grabbed it from him easily— but he was fast and he grabbed it back.

"Give it to me. Give it to me, right now!"

Max had jumped behind the blue-and-white striped chair and he was opening the envelope.

"Don't."

He opened it and peered in. He reached his hand into the envelope, picked up the key, and instantly screamed, "Oh!! Jeez!" He tossed it up in the air. Then caught it. "Oh, it's so hot," he said, kicking the blue-and-white chair, which flipped over sideways as he dropped the key onto the hardwood floor. As it hit, it seemed to set off sparks, like tiny laser beams, all the colors of the rainbow. For a fraction of a second, to Tess, it seemed to turn the bright brass color it had when it neared the gate, but then, as it fell to rest on the floor, it was once again a rusty skeleton key.

Max was stunned into silence. His index finger was bright red where the key had burned him.

"Who—Whose key is that?" he asked.

"Well," said Tess, leaning over to pick it up—she was half afraid she, too, would be burned but knew she needed to put on a show—"it's obviously not yours." Her hand folded around it. *No, just a little bit warm.* She picked up the envelope from the floor where Max had dropped it, dropped the key back into it, and folded it up.

"Where did you get that?" Max asked. "Did you find it in the attic?"

Tess didn't answer him.

"Tell me right now or I'll tell Aunt Ev." He ran for the door.

She threw her body in front of his, blocking the door. She heard her father's voice, "Please try not to be violent with each other. I know it's hard." It was something he always said to them. She summoned all her strength and self-control and stared Max down.

Now, she had another dilemma. *If someone knew a secret could you trust them not to tell? If someone didn't know the answer to a secret, could you trust them not to try to find out?*

The answer to the second question was obviously No.

"I know you didn't go bike riding Saturday," Max said. "I went to look for you and your bike was by the garage."

Tess had to admit, he had her there.

Also, she reasoned, if she was going to see William again this summer, she might need Max's help. Aunt Evie was going to think it was strange if she disappeared for hours at a time. Aunt Evie would not believe that she'd taken up poetry full-time and was sitting on the moors.

"Max, I can't . . . Set the chair upright, please, and come sit down on the bed," she said.

After they were seated, she placed the envelope like a sacred object in between them. "I can't really explain it. And if I told you the story, you might not believe it. Umm . . . but . . . see"—this was an expression she used all the time when she was little; in fact, her dad sometimes called her Miss Umbutsy. "Umm . . . but . . . see," she said again, "I think the only thing I can do is show you.

"We can't go today," she said. "Aunt Evie says it's rude to drop in on someone too often when you've only just met. But I promise, we'll go tomorrow and, when we get there, I'll ask if it's okay for you to be there, too."

"But where are we going?" asked Max.

"To my friend's house. Okay?"

There was something about the seriousness with which she said it that made Max not want to question her more.

"Pinkie swear," she said. "It's just our secret."

They linked pinkies the way they'd done when they were little, and made a solemn oath.

"Do you want to play Monopoly?" Max asked. "I promise, I won't throw the board."

"Okay," said Tess. "I'll be down in a minute."

Max left. She shut the door. She sat down on the bed for a moment to collect herself. She needed a new hiding place for the key.

an electrical storm

Tess woke up that night to a bright flash of light outside her bedroom window followed by the sound of
thunder. Lightning always made her think of her dad.
She knew she had too big an imagination. She could
imagine what it might be like to see an explosion in
the distance in the desert. She'd told him this once—
that she was afraid of lightning. He understood that it
wasn't the lightning she was afraid of. "Don't go there,"

he said. "Don't try to imagine me over there. Just think of me as right here on your shoulder. Always." She put her right hand on her own left shoulder, which is what he always did when he said it, and tried to roll over and go back to sleep.

There was another strike of lightning and another crack of thunder. Then she heard a timid knock at her door, and Max poked his head in.

"Can I—umm—hang out with you for a while?" he asked. "I can't sleep."

"Sure. I can't sleep, either."

Max lay down on top of the covers next to her.

There was another crack of lightning and then the room was plunged into darkness. Tess had carefully set the candles into the candlesticks from the antique store and put them out on top of her dresser. For a moment, she thought they were lit and that she saw a soft glow coming off of the top of the wicks.

There was another crack of lightning, this one more terrifying than the last.

"Do you do it, too?" she asked Max.

"When I hear lightning and thunder," he answered, "do I worry about Dad? Yeah." Sometimes she and Max had almost psychic communication.

"He's okay," said Tess with some confidence, taking the soft glow of the candles as a sign.

"I know," said Max. "I think we'd know it if he wasn't."

He put his head down on her pillow, shut his eyes, and fell fast asleep. Tess put her hand on his left shoulder, the way their dad would have done it if he had been there.

a visit to the castle garden

Max woke Tess up the next morning, excitedly pointing to the window. The sun was peeking out behind the clouds.

"Can we go today?" he asked without even saying, 'good morning.'

"If it's not raining. I think so," said Tess. She realized it was the first time she'd seen her brother happy in a long time. "But," she said, "let me do the talking with Aunt Evie, okay?"

As Tess was getting dressed, she noticed the candlesticks on top of her bureau and saw that the wicks of the candles were still pure-white . . . and that they'd never been lit at all. *She must have imagined it. It must've been a reflection from the lightning outside.*

For once, they all came down for breakfast at the same time.

"Let me make breakfast, Aunt Evie," Max said. It was one of the things that was unusual and endearing about Max—he loved to cook. He'd talked their mom into letting him be her sous chef when he was six and had developed excellent basic cooking skills, which extended to pancakes, spaghetti, and roast chicken. "I'll make pan-scrambled eggs," he said. "Mom says they're the best kind."

"Your grandma used to make them for us when we were little," said Aunt Evie. She set a frying pan down on the stove and handed Max a stick of butter from the fridge and a bowl with six eggs in it.

Max melted the butter over a medium flame and expertly cracked the eggs right into the sizzling butter and scrambled them up in the pan. They were a funny mixture of yellow and white and delicious.

Tess had set the table and poured juice for each of them into the jam jars that Aunt Evie used as glasses.

Aunt Evie had made toast and the three of them sat down to a breakfast that almost reminded Tess and Max of home.

"That was quite a show last night," said Aunt Evie. "Did you see it? The whole sky lit up."

"I know—it was really thrilling, wasn't it?" said Max. Tess resisted the impulse to give him a dirty look.

"I was hoping you would help me in the garden today," Aunt Evie said, "but it's too wet to garden!" Aunt Evie's back garden was a mess. It was so overgrown, it was a tangle. It definitely needed a cleaning up.

"Can we help tomorrow?" Tess asked. "We were thinking we might . . ." Tess hesitated, ". . . if it dries out a bit, take a bike ride and go on an adventure. I've never ridden due north." She pulled her compass out of the pocket of her shorts to show Aunt Evie she was prepared.

"My iPhone *has* GPS," said Max somewhat grumpily. Once a day, Max would mention something his iPhone could do that he couldn't do because there wasn't any internet service.

"It's not my fault, Max," said Aunt Evie, "that there isn't any cell service up here. I wish we had internet, too. If we had internet, I would order some tulip bulbs online."

Max and Tess started laughing. It was just like Aunt Evie to announce she wanted to go online and then figure out the most old-fashioned thing she could buy on the internet, tulip bulbs. Tess did a *Note to self: ask Mom to send Aunt Evie tulip bulbs for Christmas.*

"That sounds like fun," Aunt Evie said, already distracted by the morning paper. "I think I might make apricot jam," she announced, looking over at the counter where there was a huge basket of apricots. "Don't stay out too late. Try to be home before dark, okay?"

Victory! Tess and Max exchanged a look. "Of course, Aunt Evie," Tess answered. "Promise."

They took their bikes but didn't travel due north. They couldn't really ride them. They had to walk them up the path. Halfway up the hill, they abandoned both bicycles under a bush. When they reached the orchard, Max was surprised.

"I didn't know there was an orchard up here," he said. The orchard was pretty, some of the trees were still flowering, the others were ripe with fruit, plums, green apples, apricots. There was even a fig tree that Aunt Evie claimed she'd brought home from Greece.

"Haven't you ever been here?" Tess asked. "I come up with Aunt Evie and help her pick the fruit from the trees. Where did you think the plums and apricots came from?"

"No, I've never been here," Max answered. "And I never really thought about where the apricots came from. Is this Aunt Evie's property?"

"I think so," said Tess. She laughed. "I'm sure of it. She said she planted the fig tree, and that isn't something you'd do on someone else's property!"

Tess reached up and picked two plums from a tree. She handed a plum to Max.

He waited until she took a bite of hers before he bit into his. He had new respect for his sister after that stunt with the key.

Tess pointed to the path that stretched above the orchard and the steps cut into the rock face. Max realized his heart was beating a little quickly.

"You sure you know where we're going?"

"I think so," she said, although she thought to herself, *if it's really there*. She half expected that she had imagined it, after all.

It *was* quite a climb.

"Are you sure we haven't passed it?" Max asked. He was a little out of breath. Max sometimes got asthmatic when he ran outside. Tess realized they'd forgotten his inhaler. There wasn't any reason to bring their cell phones (or even keep them charged, as there wasn't any service) and no one had any idea where they were.

"I'll walk slower, then," she said. "Stay right behind me."

"Okay . . ."

They were at the rock face where the road seemed to change into steps cut into the cliff. "No, I remember this part," Tess said with certainty. "It's just up here a little way." Then she channeled her father, which made Max smile. "Single file. March!" she said. "Come on."

She stopped at the top of the hill, and Max, who was standing a good foot below her on the steps, couldn't see anything at all.

"Just here," she said, pointing to the gate that looked like a gingerbread cookie.

He stepped up and looked. "It's just a gate. There's nothing on either side of it," he said. "Why don't we just walk around it?"

Tess nodded. "Well . . ."

She didn't have to finish the sentence because Max tried to walk around it and his foot hit the invisible wall, then his nose touched, then his forehead, and he was thrown back onto the dirt.

She held a hand out to pull her brother up. "That would

be why," said Tess. Max's eyes were as wide as saucers.

"William says his dad has 'privacy issues,'" Tess explained. "I think it's . . ." Tess hesitated. "It must be some kind of security fence."

Max tried to figure out whether that made sense or not . . . but Tess had already pulled the skeleton key out of her pocket.

Tess turned to him and put her finger to her mouth in a gesture of 'ssshhh,' as the key once again began to spark and, as it had the first time, turned to a bright brass color as it neared the gate. The keyhole appeared out of nowhere. And as the key connected, the gate, too, transformed as if it were brand new and totally inviting.

Max broke the silence. "Wow! That was sort of in-credible."

Max was the first to peek his head in. The first thing he saw was the pond. But instead of swans, there were bullfrogs standing on the lily pads. They were big bull-frogs, practically bright green, making almost melodic, croaking noises, as if they were having a conversation with one another as they hopped from one lily pad to the next.

Tess stepped in front of Max into the garden. She looked around to see if William was there. No sign of him. She saw a lone white dove perched on the branch of a silver birch tree. And then the yellow ball came whizzing towards her. She leaned down, without missing a beat, and picked it up goalie style. She set it down on the ground before her and folded her arms on her chest.

"Good catch," he shouted to her as she shouted back, almost in unison, "Good shot. But I'm too fast for you."

He walked across the garden to her. "Is it all right," she asked, "that I brought my brother?"

"Of course it is," he answered.

"William, this is Max. Max, this is William," said Tess, making a formal introduction between them.

"Hey," said Max sheepishly.

Tess was relieved he hadn't added the word *bro* to the *hey*. Sometimes Max reverted to slang in an effort to be cool.

closet talk

If two people think something happened, did it happen?" Tess whispered even though they were sitting on the floor in the closet with the door shut.

"Stop it. You sound like Dad."

"I can't help it. I feel like Dad." This was a feeling that was partly brought on by the fact that they were having a talk in the closet. This was something their parents did in their New York apartment, as it was sort of small and privacy was hard to find. In the middle of dinner (or in the middle of the living room) sometimes either their mom or their dad would say, "Closet talk." It was like a code-word. Both of their parents would instantly retire to their bedroom, go into the closet, shut the door, and have a talk.

Tess and Max had never gone into the closet with them, so they weren't sure exactly what the procedure was. Did they talk standing up? Did they sit on the floor?

Max was SO excited when they returned to Aunt Evie's after the extraordinary afternoon at William's that Tess thought Max needed a calming down, so they could get their stories straight. "Closet talk," she said, the moment they walked in Aunt Evie's front door. And Max and Tess retired to Tess's room, went into the closet, and sat down on the floor to have a talk.

It had been an extraordinary afternoon.

a visit to the sculpture garden

here's what happened
or what they think happened,
anyway

William wasn't alone in the garden. There was a young woman in the garden sitting in a wicker chair, wearing an old-fashioned straw hat to protect her face from the sun. "Hello, I'm Marie," she said. She had a slight French accent and she extended her hand out first to Tess and then to Max as a formal hello.

Marie was either William's nanny or his governess or both. She reminded Tess of a princess in a fairy tale, but Tess couldn't quite put her finger on which fairy tale it was. Marie had blonde hair, almost the color of gold, pinned up in back but falling in front in soft curls that framed her heart-shaped face. Her eyes were blue. She had the longest lashes, even though they were also blonde, that perfectly accented her eyes. Her voice was soft and clear and she had a laugh that sounded like a bell. Her skin was pale, almost as pale as William's. She spoke three languages: French, English, and German.

She told them that she, too, had gone to a boarding school in Switzerland. "But," she laughed, "that was a long time ago." Tess didn't think it could have been too long ago—Marie didn't look that old to her, maybe 30 . . . In general, Tess thought grown-ups made way too much of their age, whatever age it was. Marie was wearing a shimmery long silvery-gray skirt, a white blouse that looked French because it had no collar, and shoes that looked like ballerina slippers. She had on very little jewelry, except Tess noticed she was wearing an antique pendant on a gold chain that curiously resembled the symbol on the skeleton key. She also had a pale, delicate sapphire ring on her left ring finger. Tess wondered if that meant she was engaged.

"I told you she'd come today," said William. "Can we show them the surprise?" he asked Marie.

Max couldn't imagine what a surprise would be, since the whole thing was so astonishing . . .

Max had his eye on the pond. But Marie, as if she'd read his mind, said, "Oh, no. We're not allowed to catch the frogs."

Max wondered whether she was some kind of eco-freak like his mom's friend Franny. He didn't really want to catch a frog—he just wanted to hold one, see it up close. Well, actually, he wouldn't mind bringing one home and convincing Aunt Evie he needed a terrarium. But he understood he had to observe "house rules," and William was already running up ahead of them.

Suddenly, they were out of the yard and in a paved area where there were ornate sculptures. Tess saw a statue of Athena, the goddess of wisdom. She knew it was Athena because there was a plaque on the face of the statue that identified her. It was a very modest sculpture garden in the sense that none of the statues were nude, no private parts visible. There were draped gowns and pantaloons carved onto the statues, some of which also had stone headdresses as if they were kings or, like Athena, gods or goddesses. Tess wanted to linger in the sculpture garden, the center-piece of which was a fountain. She wondered if that was Neptune, then she corrected herself, probably Poseidon, as he was the Greek one, the god of the sea, holding the sceptre in the middle of the fountain.

Marie was beside her. "I'm happy you like them," she said, "but we'll save our mythology lesson for another day."

"Okay," Tess told her. And then Tess yelled out to William, who had all but disappeared, "Wait up!"

William didn't have any siblings, so he wasn't accustomed to being yelled at. So, instead of being obstinate, he just obeyed instantly, stopped in his tracks, and waited for them.

Off to the left was a row of hedges. Not hawthorn, some other kind of bush. Not a row exactly, more like a construction of hedges. It did remind Tess of the maze at Hampton Court.

"It *is* a maze," said Marie, verifying Tess's thought before she could even voice it. And as she said it, Tess realized there was a connection between the word *amaze* and "a maze." Her mother always told her to look for the roots of words and this one made sense. She stopped for a minute in amazement. And then tackled Max as he was on his way toward the hedges. She could only imagine trying to explain to Aunt Evie that she had lost Max in a maze. And William had already run on ahead, and they had no choice but to follow him.

the first wish: a wild ride on a carousel

When they finally caught up to William, it was as if they were in an amusement park, or an old-fashioned version of a carnival. There was a stand painted with red-and-white stripes that looked a lot like a popcorn machine except it made doughnuts. It was automated and you could watch it through the glass as the dough puffed up and fried and became a doughnut.

A short, pleasant-looking woman with round cheeks

and absolutely no neck, wearing a white apron and a funny chef's cap, was sprinkling powdered sugar on the dough-nuts the moment they came out of the chute, then carefully sliding each into a wax paper bag. Next to her was a funny lemon tree that looked as if it had been constructed from papier-mâché. There was a faucet on its trunk that gave out fresh lemonade. Max made a dash for the doughnuts as Tess took a sip of the lemonade, but her eye was caught by what lay beyond . . .

There was a carousel, intricately carved, covered with an elaborate canopy, that had beautiful pictures painted on it, inset with tiny octagonal mirrors on its exterior that sparkled, reflecting the sun, and made it seem as if the merry-go-round itself was bathed in rainbows. Tess was utterly charmed by it. Breathless almost. There were four horses, a white one, a gray one, a brown one, and a black one that were oddly life-sized, not the usual size of a horse on a merry-go-round.

"My grandfather gave this to me on my eighth birthday." William laughed because even he knew that was ridiculous. "On special occasions, and I think this is one," he said, sort of humbly for someone who'd been given a carousel, "I'm allowed to use it."

Max put his hands on his hips and said, somewhat

tauntingly, "And what special occasion is it?" sounding a lot like Tess when he said it, Tess with an edge, a nastier version of Tess, if you will.

"Well," William answered sort of shyly, "I guess the two of you would be it," looking at Max and Tess as he said it. "I don't have company very often."

There was something about the way he said it that was sort of disarming, and even Max, who was generally protective of his older sister and understandably cautious about her new friend, would have to admit that he was starting to like William, too.

But there was still one obstacle to get past.

"Y'can't get on without a ticket." The carousel barker had a thick Irish accent. His outfit bore more resemblance to a gardener's uniform than to a carnival worker's, which made sense since his name was Barnaby, and he was actually the groundskeeper for the property. The only concession he'd made to his present assignment was a red-and-white striped ribbon he'd tied around his gardener's cap. He was a tough-looking character, his skin was weathered from days in the sun, and he looked as if he would be as much at home on the sea as he was on land, which was a good call because he had been a sailor in his youth. Max realized he wasn't someone you wanted to pick a fight with. Not that Max wanted to pick a fight. He was just a bit unsure about the carousel ride. Max thought he might be a little bit too old for merry-go-rounds but his sister, who was a year older, seemed so excited by the prospect that he had to go along.

"What do I have to do to get a ticket?" asked Max, reaching into his pocket to see if he had any coins.

"Your money's no good here, m'boy," said Barnaby. "It's your wishes I want. One wish per ride."

"You want my wish?!"

"No, m'boy. I want you to make a wish."

"I thought *you* wanted *my* wish," said Max in a somewhat softer tone of voice.

"No," Barnaby repeated. "I want *you* to make a wish!"

"Is that one wish per person or one for all of us to ride?" asked Max, his mathematical mind at work.

"Hmm, funny y'should ask that. We accept one wish for everyone to ride," he answered.

"Well, then," he said immediately, "I think I'll give the wish to my sister. Tess . . ." he called out to her. "She's the one who brought me here!" It didn't even occur to him to wonder, at first, what his wish would've been . . . and then he decided. Tess would probably wish for the same thing he would—there was only one thing they wanted.

The rules were explained. Tess was as skeptical as Max was and almost as hard on Barnaby. But he insisted, it was her wish to make. And hers to come true. She wondered if she ought to give it to William, but as if he'd anticipated the question, William said, "No, it's yours—I already got my wish today."

Tess started to say, "I wish . . ." but Barnaby stopped her.

"Oh, no," he said, practically bellowing at her. "Wishes should never be said out loud. You have to keep them a secret, otherwise they don't come true. Now close your eyes, m'girl, and make a wish."

Tess didn't think about it, certainly not as hard as Max had. She just closed her eyes and made a wish.

When she opened them, the turnstile was spinning, sort of like the revolving doors they had at that department store in New York City, slowly, so that each of them had a chance to step in and enter the carousel ride.

Tess needed a little help, which Barnaby gave her, to get her foot into the stirrup and hoist herself up onto the horse. She chose the gray horse. It was dappled and it looked as if it could use a friend. William said the black one was his. Max navigated his way onto the brown horse.

William called out, "There's four horses, Marie, come with us."

She laughed, that funny laugh she had that sounded like a bell, and said, "Okay. I will." She stepped onto the carousel, daintily picked up an edge of her flowy gray skirt, and, as if she really was a dancer, put her ballet slipper into the stirrup and hoisted herself up in one incredibly graceful move.

The music started. And that was startling, too. It was some British rock band. Tess caught some lyric about "Sailing away on a cloud in the dark of night . . ." She didn't know who the band was. She had expected *oom pah pah oom pah pah* or something that one would hear at a normal carnival, and instead it was British hard rock and completely surprising. Or as Max would say, "Totally disruptive but in a good way." Tess didn't really understand how disruptive *could* be a good thing, but in this case she almost understood.

Max was smiling again as the carousel started to turn. It was the fourth time she'd seen him smile. She looked across the carousel at William and she smiled, too. It started slowly. Round and round. It wasn't set up like a regular merry-go-round. It was as if the horses were all on separate tracks. So, as the merry-go-round began to spin faster, the horses seemed to race one another. Tess was in the lead. Now, it was going faster still.

It was going so fast, she shut her eyes for a moment. And when she opened them . . . The horses were real, at least hers and William's were no longer the wooden version on the carousel. She and William were riding across a meadow, the two horses, the gray one and the black one, running side by side, their gaits perfectly in step. Tess could hear the sound of their hoofbeats and their breath, exactly in sync with one another, as if the horses were trained to run this way, as if they were part of a funny charge across the moors. *A gallop, no, something faster than that. A canter?* She couldn't remember if that was faster or slower. *No, a gallop, a race, except they weren't racing with each other, they were just riding side-by-side.* Smoothly, almost as if they were flying, each secure in their saddle as if there was no chance of either of them falling off. William reached out to take her hand, and as their fingers touched, the horses seemed to run even faster, as if there was an electric current fueling them on. The horses were running so quickly, the landscape around them seemed almost a blur. Up ahead, Tess noticed a hedge off to the right.

She loved to ride. She couldn't help it. She let go of his hand and put both of hers on the reins. She jerked the reins just enough to steer her horse to the right, hold on, hold on, she couldn't resist it. That extraordinary feeling of being one with the horse, that felt a lot like flying, as the horse artfully jumped the hedge and landed perfectly on the other side.

Her horse slowed and came to a stop. She looked behind her to see where William was, as she assumed he would have followed her. But there was no sign of him.

The meadow seemed to have ended. There were no houses on the hillside, nothing, no trees, no doves. No grass. There was just dirt below her horse's hooves and nothing in the distance—just dirt and more dirt, as if she'd happened on a construction site where the owners hadn't yet begun the job. *That was it. That was the only logical explanation.* There was no grass, not even weeds.

Her heart was beating faster now, or still beating quickly from the ride. And she was frightened. *Had she not been supposed to jump the hedge? Had William seen her do it? Was she lost?*

She waited for what seemed like the longest time and all she heard was silence. There was only one possible solution she could think of. *If you get lost, retrace your steps.* That was something her dad had taught them when they were little. "If you get lost, retrace your steps. Go back to somewhere where someone can find you . . . if you can." He always added that part, *if you can.*

And if you can't—she didn't even want to think about that.

She laid her head down on the horse's neck. "I think I'll name you. I name you Sir—" she hesitated "—Sir Baldemare." She leaned down and stroked his mane, and whispered in the horse's ear again, "And I anoint you my knight." They were in this together, she and Sir Baldemare, and together they would escape.

She gently tugged the reins, turning the horse around. The horse was well-trained. And, at the moment, she felt that he was hers. He was her Knight and she was his Lady and together they would succeed. She whispered into the horse's ear, "Can we do it again? Can we go back where we were?"

It seemed to take the longest time. It was at least a mile, a mile of nothingness, the sky pale blue, almost as if it had no color, the absolutely flat landscape with no trace of green, until she saw the faintest speck of forest-green in the distance. She nudged the horse with her heels to make him go faster and finally saw the wall of green. She was right up against it. It was much taller than she remembered. She was somewhat surprised she'd been able to clear it before. And then she remembered something else her father had told her. "Don't ever doubt yourself." And at the same time he'd added, "But don't be fearless either." And then her dad had gone on to explain, "If you're frightened of something, figure out why. Don't be afraid to take a moment to assess the situation." At the time it had seemed to Tess like a completely useless life lesson—preposterous to think that she would ever follow in his war reporter footsteps and intentionally put herself in danger—but at this very moment, it seemed like a valuable thing to know: *take a moment to assess the situation.*

She realized there wasn't enough distance between her and the hedge. She was worried and rightly so that her horse, her knight, Sir Baldemare, might not be able to gather enough speed to jump high enough to clear the hedge. The only choice was to travel farther away again to give him more room to run . . . She was frightened to ride farther away. She realized she'd never been anywhere so desolate before. She heard her father's voice in her head: *Don't ever doubt yourself.*

There wasn't any choice. She turned Sir Baldemare around and rode back 200 yards. She turned him round again and they were facing the hedge in the distance. She leaned in and whispered to him again, "We have to go home."

She kicked him, not tentatively or randomly, a clear decisive command, as she leaned her body into his, whispering again, as she laid her head onto his neck, "We have to go home."

He started to run, then race, then cleared the hedge as artfully as he had done before.

She shut her eyes the moment he started to jump.

And when she opened them . . .

She was back on the moors, riding neck and neck with William, back the way they'd come, so quickly the landscape was a blur beside them. She shut her eyes again and Sir Baldemare seemed to slow his gait, and when she opened them, they were back on the carousel. The horses had returned to their wooden form, racing one another on the track, Sir Baldemare still in the lead, the rock song blaring in the background. As the merry-go-round slowed to a halt, the music stopped, almost as if it was cued to end, the way a music box does the moment it stops spinning.

William held his head up high as he dismounted.

Max looked a bit dizzy but Max couldn't even ride in the front seat of a car without getting carsick. He had to be helped down by Barnaby.

Marie's hair was falling, her face truly framed by golden curls. She looked like she'd stepped out of a painting as she artfully swung her left leg over her right and landed as if she'd done an entrechat, an antic dance move where you cross your feet twice before you land.

Tess, trying to slow her heartbeat, put her head down on Sir Baldemare's neck, then proudly dismounted. She was the last to exit the turnstile. And as she did, Barnaby said to her, under his breath, "I thought we'd lost you there for a minute."

Tess smiled at him and said, "I'm not that easy to lose."

Barnaby tipped his gardener's cap to her and said, "I can see that, M'Lady."

an invitation
to dinner

They walked back through the sculpture garden. Not one of them said a word. Tess was enormously relieved when they reached the backyard and there was the perfectly mown lawn. The frogs were chirping in the pond and jumping back and forth on the lily pads.

It must've been a construction site. That was the only thing she could think of. *Someone had levelled*

*the land and hadn't yet started to build. But that didn't
account for the silence . . .*

Max was looking a little green. He really did have
motion sickness. The doughnut lady offered him a glass
of lemonade, which she said was excellent for settling
stomachs. It turned out her name was Clarissa and she was
really the cook. She'd made lovely shortbread cookies,
cream puffs, and petits fours with pink and green icing. Tess
was starving and proceeded to eat three cream puffs, two
shortbread cookies, and five petits fours, at which point
Marie gave her a look that clearly stated that perhaps she'd
eaten enough! Tess put a half-eaten cookie down. "I have a
terrible sweet tooth," she confessed. "I always have."

Max insisted he couldn't eat anything because he was
dizzy from the merry-go-round.

"The carousel wasn't the hardest part," said Tess. Max
looked at her confused. Tess realized that he didn't know
what she was referring to . . .

The sun had moved again in the sky. Tess knew they
had to head back home. She took a last look at the garden.
She hadn't noticed all the white roses in a bed next to the
hydrangeas edging the perfectly green lawn. Her mother
loved white roses.

She took a walk over to the rose garden and leaned

down to smell their fresh and fragrant scent. *Pure Oxygen,* her mother would've said.

William had walked with her to the rose bed. "I would give you one," he said, "but we're not allowed to cut the roses." Somehow the fact of another rule didn't surprise Tess at all. She thought it was sweet of William to want to give her a rose.

Tess was so grateful to be back on planted ground. She looked around the yard. There was the white tablecloth on the grass, the wicker basket for the sweets, the silver birch tree that now had two white doves resting on its branches.

"It's so beautiful here," said Tess.

"You should see it at night," said William, "when the stars are out!"

William ran across the lawn to Marie. Tess started to run after him. She realized her legs were sore from the ride as she couldn't quite run as fast as him. She'd wanted to ask him about the hedge, about the house next door, or the not house next door, but he was already off on the next thing.

"Marie," he said excitedly, "could we invite Tess and Max for dinner? Not tonight, properly, as if it was a party. Three people's enough for a party, isn't it? I mean four . . . Could we have a party Saturday night?"

Marie laughed and looked at Tess for a response.

"We would have to ask Aunt Evie if it's all right," Tess answered. "We've never gone out on our own at night, not since we've been in England. She would probably insist on driving us."

Barnaby, who was standing a few feet away eating the last of a cream puff, piped in, "Tell her I'll be happy to drop you back!"

"Is there a proper address?" Max asked. "I mean, a front door."

It was so like Max to think of something logical like that.

Barnaby answered again. "Of course there is. Just drive up to the gate. 200 Hampshire Road. I'll let you in."

That made sense. Aunt Evie's address was 100 Hampshire Road. Tess found it sort of reassuring that there was a front entrance, after all.

As they were about to leave through the back gate, William whispered in her ear, "But be sure to bring the key. You never know when we might need it."

Tess looked at him curiously and nodded. There *were* so many questions she wanted to ask but it was late and if their aunt approved, she would see him Saturday . . .

*wondering if
they might have
imagined it,
after all...*

They raced down the hill, through the orchard, and back to their aunt's, Tess complaining all the way that her legs were stiff. When they entered the house, Max was flushed from the carousel ride and the run down the hill. He, too, was understandably full of questions. Most of which Tess didn't think she could answer, and some of which she thought they'd best keep from their aunt, which is why she'd announced a "closet talk" and she and Max were sitting on the floor of her closet with the door shut.

"Who is William?" asked Max. "Do you know anything about him?" Tess thought he sounded so much like their father. She realized how protective Max was of her. Funny, her younger brother showing what her dad would call his protective stripes.

He went on to ask, "I mean, what is the castle exactly?" before she could even answer the first two. "When do you think it was built?"

"Do you think it really is a castle?" Tess answered. "Or just a big house?"

Tess realized she'd never been inside the castle. The two times she'd been there, she'd only been outside. She had a lot of questions, too.

"If it's just a big house, it's in the design of a castle."

"Okay," said Tess, "fair enough."

"And whose castle is it? Is it theirs? Aunt Evie thought they were summer renters."

"It seems to be, doesn't it?" said Tess. "Their castle. I mean, William said his grandfather gave the merry-go-round to him as a birthday gift. It sounds like it belongs to his family."

"I guess that's right," Max answered. "That makes

sense. I sure understand what it's like to have your dad be away."

Tess hesitated. "Were you worried when I disappeared?" she asked.

Max looked at her completely puzzled.

"When?"

"When we were riding on . . ."

Max interrupted her, "The carousel? Did you disappear?"

She realized that he didn't know what she was talking about. She started to describe the meadow and then something about the way Max looked at her—as if she was out of her mind—made her stop. She did wonder if it had been her wish all along.

What if it was true? What if wishes did come true and she'd wasted a wish, a real wish . . . Why hadn't she wished for something more—something more than a ride on a real horse?

But her dad always said things happened the way they were supposed to and that you weren't supposed to feel regret. She understood that, now. It was the first time she'd ever felt regret, selfish, that she'd wished it was a real horse, something so trivial and momentary, and that she and William were going for a real ride. She should have wished for something so much more. But maybe she had imagined it, after all.

If you could make a real wish, what would it be? Tess knew what hers was.

Their conversation was interrupted by a brisk knock, three times on the door.

"Yoo-hoo!" Aunt Evie called out as she opened the closet door and saw the two of them sitting on the floor having what appeared to be a deep conversation.

"Hmm," she said, "I was wondering where you were . . ."

"Umm . . . we were ummm, playing a game called 'spy'," said Tess in an attempt to explain why they were sitting on the floor of the closet. "It always starts in the closet."

Max was impressed his sister came up with that so fast.

"We used to play it with Dad sometimes," Tess added.

"Oh," said Aunt Evie, "that's very creative. Dinner's ready. Didn't want it to get cold." She turned and walked out of the room so quickly, they had no choice but to follow her down the stairs to the dining room.

After they were all seated at the table and Aunt Evie had said grace, "Bless us every one and all the ones we love," folded her napkin in her lap, and served them each a slice of chicken, mashed potatoes, and peas, she asked, "What was your afternoon like?"

"Lovely," said Tess.

"Where were you exactly?" asked Aunt Evie.

"At William's," said Tess.

And Max added, just to be precise, "200 Hampshire Road."

"Really?" said Aunt Evie. "200 Hampshire Road? Are you sure that address is right?"

Max and Tess both nodded.

"The old Bramsfield Castle? Really. No one's lived there for years. Really?"

Aunt Evie said "Really?" about four more times until Tess finally said, "Yes, Aunt Evie, we're sure that's the right address. Max and I both know it because he invited us for dinner Saturday night."

There was a slight pause before Aunt Evie said, "Really?"

"Really," said Tess. "Honestly. Really."

Tess poured Max a glass of water from the pitcher on the table since he still looked sort of green. "Thanks, Tess," he muttered and then took a tiny sip.

"I thought the castle was abandoned. That they hadn't

been able to find any of the heirs. That's so curious," Aunt Evie said. "Since I've been coming here with John for summers"—Aunt Evie had a curious habit of referring to her dead husband in the present tense—"over twelve years now, no one's lived there. Hmmm. I wonder if the magistrate has taken it over, then? Are they renters?"

"What's a magistrate?" asked Max as he pushed his peas around on his plate so Aunt Evie might think he was eating.

"You know," said Tess, "someone official like the State of New York."

"Oh," said Max. "I don't know about that, but it doesn't seem as if they're renters. He seems to be part of the family that owns the home. He says it used to be his grandfather's house. His father's in London, though, and he's here with his governess."

"She's French," Tess said quickly. "Her name's Marie. But her English is perfect. And she seems to take good care of him. There's also a groundskeeper named Barnaby. And I think he lives there, too."

"And a cook," Max added.

"They must've come into some money, then. I thought the place was in disarray."

"The gardens are beautiful," said Tess. "A perfect

lawn, a bed of white roses, a pond with swans and," she looked at Max, "bullfrogs. A very well-tended garden. In fact, it inspired us. Can we help you in your garden tomorrow? The roses really are a bit of a tangle. And your rosemary's way overgrown."

Aunt Evie couldn't help but smile at Tess's knowledge of a garden, which fell into the category for her of "things that are passed down to you by your mother."

"But," Tess continued, "I think if Max and I attack the rose bushes—Mother taught us how, we always help her in the country—we might be able to get them to bloom again. I bet there's other things hidden in there, too. Kind of like your own secret garden."

"It's true," Aunt Evie answered. "There used to be lovely lilies. The bulbs should still be there and Lord knows what else. I could use the help."

"Can we?" Tess asked.

"Can you what?" said Aunt Evie, who'd lost the thread of the conversation, as she was trying to remember where she'd planted the hydrangeas and if any of them even had the faintest blooms.

"Can we go to William's for dinner Saturday?" asked Tess. Then she looked at her brother, who hadn't touched his food. "Try the mashed potatoes, Max. You always like those. We ate too much at William's house today. The cook made home-made petits fours."

"Really?!" said Aunt Evie. At which point Tess and Max couldn't help it. They both started laughing for reasons they couldn't quite explain.

aunt evie's garden

What's a crocus?" asked Max.

"It's a little blue flower," Tess said.

"I think I found one," Max said.

"Really?" said Tess, inadvertently doing a perfect imitation of Aunt Evie when she said it.

At which point Max and Tess broke into uncontrollable laughter again. Luckily, for both of them, Aunt Evie smiled.

They were helping her in the garden—her garden—although it was such a tangle, it was hard to call it a garden at first.

"Oh dear," said Aunt Evie when they first went into the backyard. "I have no idea how I'd do this if the two of you weren't here!" She gave them each a pair of gardening gloves, a small trough, and eXpert gardening shears, at least that's what it said on the handle: eXpert. "Be careful with those," Aunt Evie said. "Be sure to lock them and unlock them and watch out for your fingers!"

Tess could've quoted the next thing she said, pointing to the roses. "Cut above a five-leaf cluster." It was something their mom always said, "Cut above a five-leaf cluster. Roses have three-leaf clusters and five-leaf clusters." And you were supposed to cut just above the five-leaf cluster. It was supposed to encourage growth, or at least that was the common belief in the family. There was only one problem—a lot of the roses didn't have leaves at all. But Aunt Evie, anticipating the dilemma, added, "Unless, of course, they don't really have any leaves. Just cut them anywhere above a notch and maybe they'll sprout something. Maybe . . ." Aunt Evie didn't sound too sure.

Evie was upset that she had let the garden get so overgrown. It was one of the things she'd always done with her husband, John—trim the garden, he would mow the lawn—and it was the one thing she couldn't bear to do alone. The morning glories had quite tangled themselves around almost everything in the garden.

"Just pull them out," Aunt Evie instructed. "Clip them somewhere and just keep pulling. Watch out for the rose thorns. And don't throw the morning glories back in the dirt. They'll simply root again. Toss them over on this sheet I laid out on the lawn."

In truth, you could hardly call it a lawn. It looked more like a meadow. Aunt Evie thought the most they would be able to do is pull some weeds from it and let the funny flowers grow wild—as if she had her own version of a moor. But Max surprised her and pulled the lawn mower out of the shed.

"Don't worry, Aunt Evie. Dad taught me how to do this. The one we have in the country runs on gas. But this one looks like it just runs on its own."

Aunt Evie laughed. "Well, it would hardly run on its own. At least I don't think it could. It kind of needs you to push it," which, she had to admit, Max was doing quite efficiently.

"If you're going to William's on Saturday night for dinner," Aunt Evie announced, "I think I'll go into town to The White Horse." She dropped her voice to a whisper, "They have a poker game in the back room on Saturday nights."

"Real money?" asked Max.

"Yep," said Aunt Evie, "but don't tell anyone, it's probably not legal."

Aunt Evie was lying to them, but they didn't know that. She wasn't going to The White Horse at all. In fact, if things worked out the way they were supposed to, she would have quite a surprise in store for the children. Since, in her experience, though, things didn't always turn out the way they were supposed to, she thought it was best if she kept it a secret for now. Aunt Evie had a few tricks up her sleeve, too. But all she said out loud was, "An evening out sounds splendid."

"Is that a yes, then?" asked Tess. "Can we go to William's?" Tess realized Aunt Evie had never quite answered the question the night before.

"You mean, *may* we," said Aunt Evie. "And that was a yes."

trying to find
the meaning of the
hawthorn trees

Aunt Evie fell asleep on the living room sofa after supper. Tess tiptoed out of the living room and into the study. She pulled the big *Encyclopedia of Plants and Herbs* down from the bookshelf and sat down on the floor. Tess thought there was something Aunt Evie hadn't told them about the hawthorn trees—her face had darkened and she'd said something like, "Oh, this is very complicated," and shut the book. In Tess's mind that was just grown-up code for: Oh, this is something children don't need to know. Tess wanted to know everything she could about hawthorn trees and why William had warned her to stay away from them.

There it was. Oh, it was complicated and somewhat contradictory. And . . . and, she had to admit, a little scary.

Hawthorn can bring good luck or bad luck. It flowers in May, but it is thought to be unlucky to bring a flowering branch into the house; the mother of the house might die. The book actually said that. It also said, *If you sit under a hawthorn tree on the first of May, then you were likely to be spirited away to the fairy world forever.* Luckily, thought Tess, it was long past May, so they didn't have to worry about that one. *The Pilgrims named their ship after it, the* Mayflower. That was the sort of trivia her dad would probably appreciate. But it also said, *Hawthorn has long been thought to be the cure for broken hearts.* Tess had no idea what that could even mean. Did that mean that it was actually used as medicine, like if someone had had a heart attack or something, or that it could cure a romantically broken heart? She shut the book and put it back up on the shelf, carefully, so that Aunt Evie would never know she had taken it down. Good luck or bad luck? It was very confusing. In any event, Tess resolved to try her best to stay away from the hawthorn trees . . .

entering the castle from the front door

I think my car would look lovely parked in their drive-way, don't you?" said Aunt Evie when they pulled up to the gates at Bramsfield Castle. Max started laughing. "I don't remember it being so grand," she said.

It was just after seven and still light out. The gates were imposing and Tess noticed a crest in the middle of them, the same symbol that was in the skeleton key now resting safely in the black sequined evening bag she'd borrowed from Aunt Evie. She wondered if that was the best place for it. There wasn't a pocket in her black pencil skirt. There wasn't a pocket in the white silk sleeveless blouse she had on. She was wearing boots, tie-up boots, that she loved, black suede. She opened the purse and took the key out and instinctively put it in her boot, as if she was a warrior going into battle. Or a spy. She could hear William's voice—*be sure to bring the key.*

"What sort of architecture is that?" asked Tess.

"Definitely Gothic," said Aunt Evie. The castle was almost black and the metalwork extraordinarily ornate. "I don't see the bell," said Aunt Evie. "I mean, there should be a call box or something."

Max got out of the car. "I see a bell," he said, pointing to the top of the gate.

In fact, there was an old-fashioned bell. It seemed to be made of bronze, although it too had blackened. It was hanging at the top of the gate with a long braided rope cord trailing down from it.

Max shrugged at them, like *what the heck*, pulled on it, and the bell swung from right to left and back again, from right to left and back again . . . It sounded almost like church bells echoing against the moors. It sounded almost like the beginning of a symphony . . .

Tess didn't know a lot about music, but she recognized that whatever these chords were, they must be in minor, discordant and oddly inviting at the same time. Then, suddenly, there was a tap-tap-tapping, as if someone was knocking on a door or there was a bass line to the bells. Tess was starting to think William's father had a strange sense of humor.

As the bells began to ring, with that funny underlying drumbeat, the lights in the lampposts on the gates came on. *Well, were they lights?* They looked like candles in glass boxes and, almost as if it were on a timer sequence, the exterior of the castle lit up, as did the interior, so that it no longer looked quite so foreboding. Especially since that strange soundtrack was still emanating from the bell.

A moment later, Tess could just make out the figure of Barnaby in the shadow of the lamppost on the left side of the gate. He was wearing his gardener's gear, but he'd put on a top hat and a black silk vest over his shirt in an effort to be elegant or festive.

He walked over to the car. "You must be Aunt Evie. Pleased to meet you. I've heard a lot about you. I'm Barnaby. Keeper of the grounds. I promise I'll take good care of them, deliver them home by ten. I'd invite you in," he said, "but I don't think your car would make it over the drawbridge. It needs a bit of repair. The drawbridge,

I mean, not your car. I keep my buggy outside," he added.

"Is there water under the drawbridge?" Aunt Evie asked.

"Of course there is," was the reply.

"Hmm," said Aunt Evie. "I thought the water dried up some years ago," she said almost to herself. It had rained a bit this last winter, but she did think that the creek bed had gone dry.

"William's father's still in London," said Barnaby, "or I would ask you in to meet him."

Aunt Evie was dying to see the inside of the castle, but she thought it would be rude to insist. Tess had scrambled out of the car already. She and Max were standing at Barnaby's side. In her mind, Aunt Evie calculated how long her own evening might last.

"It's okay," she said, after a bit of a pause, "if you drop them at eleven. Going out to . . ."—she hesitated—"dinner myself. After all, it is Saturday night."

Barnaby agreed. "Saturday night, indeed," he said. "The moon's full tonight. Think it's a blue one and—"

Max interrupted without letting Barnaby finish. "It *is* a blue moon. A blue moon is when there are two full moons in a month." Max was proud of himself for knowing this fact.

"Yes," said Barnaby, "but it's also a blood moon, a total lunar eclipse. And a blood moon is something that doesn't happen very often. It's strange to have a blue moon and a blood moon on the same night."

Max butted in, "It's also a super moon tonight, that's when the moon is at its closest point to the earth."

"It's very rare to have them all on the same night," said Barnaby sounding a little bit spooky. "It's a very special night indeed," he declared.

Before Tess could even consider whether this was ominous or not, Aunt Evie started to hum the melody to the classic old song "Blue Moon," totally embarrassing Max and Tess. But Barnaby just grinned. And Tess thought she even saw him wink at Aunt Evie.

As Aunt Evie backed out of the driveway, Barnaby waved good-bye. He put his hand on the gatepost, and almost the moment he touched it, the gate to the castle swung open from the center, both sides, slowly and grandly. Curiously though, when Tess looked at the gatepost, she didn't see any button he could've pushed. William's father sure was a stickler for security.

"Are there fish?" Tess asked. She thought she saw something silver and shimmery glide through the water underneath the drawbridge.

"Mmm, silver fish," said Barnaby. "Lots of them. There's no fishing allowed on the property."

That didn't surprise Tess. She knew they were eco-freaks. Although she didn't quite know what a silver fish was, she thought it was some kind of a bug . . . maybe he was just referring to their color.

"There are probably snakes," said Max, in a spooky voice as if he was trying to frighten her.

"If I find a python, I'll bring it to you," said Tess. She was sort of annoyed. He'd been so nice for most of the week. Tess wasn't surprised that he chose that moment to be "disruptive," to use one of his favorite expressions. Max really did like to be the center of attention and that wasn't likely this evening. Also, it occurred to her, her brother might be a little nervous, too. The castle was sort of daunting.

Barnaby shook his head. "I've been here for years," he said. "I've never seen a snake on the property. It isn't the snakes we worry about."

Tess was just about to ask what he was worried about when the front door swung open, revealing a kind of grandeur she'd never seen before.

There was a knight in the entryway. Tess was startled as she almost bumped into it. He was holding a dark axe, double sided, double-edged, that looked as if it could do some damage.

"Don't worry," said Barnaby. "It's not a real knight," as he lifted up the helmet mask to show her it was empty. "It's not a knight, really," he said. "It's just a knight's armor. And, of course, his weapon." *A knight was never dressed without his sword or axe.* Tess remembered that from Middle Ages class. She was awfully glad they weren't in the Middle Ages any more.

William was standing on the landing of the stairs. He was wearing trousers and suspenders, but on him they looked sort of hip.

Tess realized she might have a crush on William. She felt her cheeks turn pink, which Max, of course, noticed, as William walked down the stairs to join them.

She hoped Max wasn't going to do anything tonight to embarrass her. He could be completely oblivious to other people's feelings.

Max didn't even realize that all the girls at school had a crush on him—even the older girls. He was completely unaware of the way they looked at him. He lived in his own world, fascinated by facts, occasionally kind and sometimes awful. Their mom said he was only mean when he was insecure. Tess reckoned the grandeur of the castle itself might be enough to make anyone insecure. Partly to manipulate Max and partly because she, too, was a little in awe of the castle, she whispered to him, "If you see a real knight, will you protect me?"

Max held his right pinkie up, which was their public version of a pinkie swear. Tess held hers up back at him.

the porcelain doll, the car collection, and table hockey

William invited them upstairs in his room to "idle" before dinner. That's the word he used. "It's cosier there," he said as he led them up what Tess instantly dubbed, *the extremely, incredibly, big, long staircase.* The stairs themselves were carpeted with a rug that was so ornate and lush and intricately patterned that Tess thought it must be Chinese or French, definitely museum quality. Max, meanwhile, counted the stairs as they walked up them—the staircase angled twice—42 steps. He tried to calculate how high the ceiling was.

On the second floor (or was it the third floor), there was an exceptionally long hallway that went in both directions.

William made a right turn towards his room. Tess wondered if there was an attic as well as a dungeon. She imagined it might be easy to get lost in the castle and that it could be difficult to be found.

"How many bedrooms are there?" asked Tess.

William hesitated. "I'm not sure," he said shyly. That was one of the nice things about William. He didn't brag about what he had . . . not like some of the kids she'd met at school in Switzerland.

"I bet you wish it had room numbers sometimes," she said.

Tess bit her lip. It had probably been a rude remark. It was an attempt at a joke but nobody laughed. *Note to self: think before you speak, especially when you're nervous.*

"No," he said quite frankly. "I wish we had more guests. When my grandfather was alive, more people came to visit us."

His bedroom was at the very end of the hallway, with windows on three sides. It was more like a suite than a bedroom. It had a sitting room/playroom and then a very large bedroom with a fireplace and a double bed. There were French doors which opened out onto a balcony on which was an ornate metal table and four chairs. There was a view of the garden and the countryside beyond. There was a crimson comforter on the bed, an embroidered headboard, and an enormous amount of pillows. It was very grand. She noticed that he didn't have a television. There was, however, a very beautiful bookshelf. Everything on it looked like it was a first edition. She wondered if he had a first edition of *The Boy's King Arthur*. It probably had beautiful color illustrations.

There was a porcelain doll on a shelf. She was very beautiful, in a white dress, with a perfectly painted face and the most delicate hands that also seemed to have polish on the nails. "My grandfather gave her to me," William explained. "She was my mother's doll when she was little. She has a trick. Do you want to see it?"

William didn't wait for them to answer. He took down a circular brown stand on the shelf next to the doll. There was a metal spike sticking up from the center and William carefully slipped her down so that the metal piece attached to the porcelain doll's back. He held it up and turned it sideways and Tess and Max could see there was a tiny screw on the bottom of the round wood saucer like the winding key of a music box. William wound it and carefully set the doll down on the table. Tchaikovsky's music to *Swan Lake* started to play and the porcelain doll seemed almost to come to alive, as it moved the moment the music started, and began to perform twirls and arabesques and, at the very end, an excellent plié to the "floor" with a bow.

"Wow. I didn't expect her to do that," said Tess. "That was lovely." Tess did a little spin of her own while William disengaged the doll from the base and put her carefully back up on the shelf.

Max was already distracted by William's very cool collection of antique cars, including a 1932 Ford with real leather seats. "Is it okay to touch them?" asked Max, who for a change was being more polite than his sister.

"Of course," said William. "This is my favorite." He pointed to a silver Aston Martin, which he then casually handed to Max.

But Max's eye was on the table hockey. Max loved table hockey. He'd become quite skilled at it at boarding school. Tess had long given up being any good at it, so, she watched while Max beat William the first game. And then William surprised Max and turned out to be a terror on his own.

The score was one–one when Barnaby bellowed up

the stairs that dinner was served. His voice seemed to echo, almost as if it came through a loudspeaker in the walls. "There's an intercom, right?" said Max.

William looked at him puzzled, as if he hadn't understood the question, as Max unsuccessfully scanned the room for any evidence of speakers in the walls.

"Come on, then," Barnaby bellowed again, and the three of them half ran down the long hallway and down the stairs.

a dance before dinner

Tess hesitated in the door of the dining room. Stars strung on garlands hung, like upside-down rainbows, from the tops of the window frames. They were prisms, carefully carved, multi-faceted, almost like diamonds, in varying sizes of five-point stars. Reflected through their glass, patches of multicolored light in geometric patterns seemed to sparkle on the parquet floor. Tess had an impulse to do a dance on one of them but resisted.

Well, she thought she resisted. But then the strangest thing happened . . .

She saw an image of herself doing a dance on one of them. She reached down and pinched her thigh to make sure she was still there. She was still there. Standing in the doorway of the dining room. But there was also a perfect image of her dancing on the parquet floor, seemingly surrounded in a halo of multi-colored light. And she could hear music. The music stopped and then she heard applause.

Oh dear, she thought, *I really am imagining things.* But William had the most curious smile on his face, as if he had seen it, too.

She'd heard about things like this, that you could step in some place and maybe never return. *No, no, it had just been her imagination. And everything looked right again.* The dining room looked very formal, despite its festive star-like decorations. There were heavy floral drapes pulled back, tucked into sconces, and tied with golden rope. The dining room table, with wood-carved high-backed chairs, looked as if it seated 20 or maybe more. There was the crest again, carved into the back of each chair. The table was covered in a white tablecloth with lace edging. There was a bowl of peaches and nectarines as a centerpiece, artfully arranged with another star prism set into it for effect.

Max had already stepped into the dining room and was just about to take a bite of a peach. Tess appreciated it that her brother was acting normally and behaving as if he felt comfortable in the castle. Tess followed his lead and walked into the dining room, as well.

There were three places set at the end of the table—one at the head and one on each side. Tess didn't know much about china except she could tell it was fancy. One plate rested on a larger plate. The underneath plate had a gold rim. She was certain the silverware was real silver. She picked up a fork and wasn't surprised that it had the same symbol in it as the key she remembered was safely in her boot, and the back of the chair she was sitting in.

Tess couldn't imagine what it would be like to live in such a big house alone. No wonder William wished he had more company. Of course there were all the people who took care of him, Marie, Barnaby, and Clarissa, who, it turned out, also had a daughter named Clara. Clara was six feet tall, plain-faced, with dark hair that was pulled back in an unruly bun. Clara was somewhat awkward herself in the formal black uniform with a white apron she was wearing while she served them dinner.

After Clara went back into the kitchen, Max, as usual, broke the ice. "Don't you think it's funny," Max whispered, "that she named her daughter after herself?"

Tess smiled. William looked baffled.

"Clara, Clarissa—she just dropped the 'iss'," said Max.

Tess had known exactly what he was talking about. It was so like Max to figure something like that out. Clara, Clarissa, you just drop the "iss."

"I think it's sort of great," Tess said. She hesitated. "Don't you think it's weird," she added, "that only boys can be juniors or seconds or thirds? I've never thought that was fair. Although I don't think it would be fair if I named my daughter Tess Barnes II, to my daughter or my husband, since her last name probably wouldn't be Barnes, right?"

Max started laughing. "If you named your daughter Tess Barnes II, I would call her 'deuce.'"

"Thanks, Max."

William marvelled at the way they communicated with one another. "I'm a third," he said shyly. "William Bramsfield III. Although I never use it. Well, that's not true—it's on my stationery."

He was a third and he had engraved stationery. It occurred to Tess that her dad was right about very rich people. They were sort of different from the rest of us.

The dinner itself wasn't particularly fancy except for the presentation. There were fresh vegetables cut into the shape of flowers, radishes and turnips, and curlicues of carrots and celery served with a fresh onion dip that wasn't nearly as zippy as Lipton's.

There were delicious shepherd's pies made with pheasant—okay, it was a little fancy—and fresh peas.

William suggested they have dessert and tea in the garden. "The moon is full," he said.

"We heard that," Tess answered. "And it's a blue moon."

"I think it might be a red one, too," William replied.

"A blood moon, y'mean," said Barnaby, who was standing in the doorway of the kitchen waiting to take them outside.

"What time is the eclipse tonight?" asked Max. He wished he had his iPhone so he could check. "Will we be able to see the eclipse from here?" he added before anyone could even answer his first question, since he remembered eclipses could only be seen from certain geographic spots depending on the time of year.

"You'll definitely be able to see the eclipse from here," said Barnaby. And then he added, his voice dropping almost an octave, "Sometimes objects have to pass each other in order for the world to be right."

Tess thought there was something menacing in the way he'd said this. She wished she had *her* iPhone. She wanted to see what time the eclipse was. She sort of hoped they'd be home before it happened.

Tess was surprised Marie talked to Barnaby that way.

But Barnaby came right back at her. "They know I'm their biggest defender."

"Whose? The gods or the children?" asked Marie.

"Well, I guess both of 'em," said Barnaby. "Sometimes when we were at sea, we used to pray to Poseidon to guide us when there wasn't a moon or the stars to tell direction from. That wouldn't be the case tonight," he added, pointing up to the stars.

"Just to the north of the Big Dipper," said Barnaby, "is the North Star. The North Star is due north," he added, pointing to the North Star. "So, that way," he gestured behind him, "would be south, and that way," he threw his arm out to the right, "would be east. And that way," he threw his left arm out to the left, "would be west." Tess had to resist the impulse to giggle.

"And that's, also, my impersonation of a compass," said Barnaby, just to prove he had a sense of humor, too.

The statue of Poseidon was in the middle of the fountain, holding a trident that seemed to be painted gold or else it was real gold. The tips of the prongs were almost red, as if lightning could come out of them. Tess realized she was letting her imagination run away with her again.

But then, Athena's eyes seemed to glisten and throw

off blue sparks, and Barnaby pointed to the sky. "That there's the Pleiades," he said, pointing to the seven-star constellation, "the seven stars. The Seven Sisters."

The moon had risen higher in the sky, casting an even brighter glow. In the sculpture garden, Athena's eyes turned a darker blue, the sapphires seemed to sparkle and then shot out sparks. The blue sparks turned to beams, almost like lasers, shooting straight up directly to the sky.

Poseidon's trident turned a brighter red and threw off three golden rays that also shot directly toward the stars.

The yellow rays and blue rays criss-crossed as they raced at rocket speed. Their color changing, so at times it seemed as if they were the entire color spectrum, a light show in the night, red, blue, purple, yellow, green, white, bright white, lighting the sky like an explosion. The beams of light raced toward the stars, with clear direction, straight for the constellation of the Pleiades. The Seven Sisters.

The Pleiades were bathed in a blue and orange glow that turned to purple, setting them off from the other stars as if there was a spotlight on them and they were onstage.

"That there's Maia," said Barnaby, pointing to one of

the seven stars, "the oldest sister. Watch 'er take the lead."

It was as if there was a giant flashlight blazing on the stars, almost a telescopic view of the one constellation. And in return, the stars of the Pleiades themselves sparkled brightly and seemed to take the shape of young girls or ballerinas.

At the same time, Tess felt as if she, too, were bathed in light. She looked down and she was wearing a strangely flowy costume, in muted colors of pink and beige, panels of silk and chiffon at the skirt, so that her legs could poke through, as if she were dressed like a ballerina or a fairy. There was a spotlight all around her and the light felt like a pathway to the stars.

Tess watched as, led by the oldest si Maia, the stars in the shape of young girls now seemed to bre into a dance, as Barnaby had predicted.

And then she watched as the bright light that enclosed her became a straight chute up to the stars and she felt herself lifted, as if by invisible strings, and she danced onto the night sky and took Maia's place on the line. She led them, the other stars in the shape of sprite-like spirited ballerinas, faster, as if they were nymphs, dancing, twirling, the panels of their skirts like ribbons in the sky, each glissade, each entrechat, each jump, leaving stardust in its wake, like a synchronized display of lights, or sparkles from a fairy's wand. And there was music, the lightest music in the world, flute music, or was it coming from a high-pitched keyboard, with the accompaniment of a harp, melodic, with sharp bells instead of a rhythm base. And then it was silent and the girls changed back to their star-like form and returned silently to their original constellation, as Tess stared up at them and wondered if she'd ever left the ground at all.

William's response was cryptic and difficult to interpret. "Impressive," he said, just that one word.

Tess looked at Max to see if he had seen it, too. "Wow," said Max, another one-word response, which didn't really answer her question either . . .

"Strange things happen," said Barnaby, "when there's a blue moon."

As they walked back to the garden, Tess said to Max, under her breath, "Logical explanation?"

"High-tech fireworks display," he answered. But it sounded more like a question than an answer . . .

Tess was too afraid to ask the real question. *Had Max seen her dancing, too?*

She looked down and she was wearing a white blouse, a black pencil skirt, no dance costume at all. But when she took a step, she saw just a trace of something that looked like white sparkles or stardust, glancing off the heel of her black suede lace-up boot, leaving a slight glittery trail behind her. Or else, she'd just been staring at the stars too long.

the rules
of the game

There was another surprise waiting for them in the garden. Set up on the lawn was the funniest version of a miniature golf game, well, sort of a miniature golf game. There was a miniature of the castle gates, and then a drawbridge, a funny facade of the castle itself and an entrance to the castle, a hallway to the conservatory, a miniature of the backyard, including a miniature pond with papier-mâché swans and frogs on lily pads. There were four mallets painted with barber-pole swirls of color on them, one red, one blue, one purple, one green, and matching balls that were absolutely round, more like billiard balls than golf balls.

"I always play the blue," said William, "is that okay?"

"I'll take the red," said Max.

"Excellent," said Tess. "I want the purple. But first, I want some ginger cake."

Tess had a theory about competitive sports and psyching out your opponents. But first you had to size up your opponents. Rule one: Make them feel as if you're in command. Hence the ginger cake demand. *Her timing. Her rules.* It was a ridiculous theory. Even she realized that. But it might be the only advantage she had. She was good at soccer, not bad at paddle tennis, and pretty much unskilled at golf. She'd never even been on a real golf course.

She hated to lose though. Tess realized her dad was right and William had already busted her on it, too—she was really competitive.

"Marie, do you want to play, too?" asked William. "There's an extra mallet." He called it a mallet, not a club, but it did look more like a mallet.

"No," said Marie, "I'll sit this one out. You three go ahead."

"I'll be umpeer," said Barnaby. He meant to say *umpire*, but his accent mangled it and Tess and William and Max all started laughing.

"It is not smart," said Barnaby, "to laugh at the umpeer!"

Barnaby put a helmet on but didn't put the face guard down, so now he looked like a weird auto mechanic or an inventor, which caused Max and Tess to start to laugh again.

"I'm sorry," said Tess. "I'm really sorry." She did not want the umpeer to be mad at her!

"What are the rules?" asked Max.

"We don't play the way other people do," said William.

"That doesn't surprise me," said Tess.

William smiled at her. It was one of the things she liked about him. She could say something terrible or caustic, and he wasn't ever mad at her. He got the joke. *It was nice to have friends who understood you, didn't think you were being rude just because you were forthright. It was nice to have friends who liked you.*

"When one person clears a hurdle," William went on to explain, "everyone moves ahead. But *only* the person who cleared the hurdle gets the point. It's more fun to stay together. You get three balls, so, if you knock one into the

water under the drawbridge or something else happens"—
he exchanged a pointed look with Barnaby—"you still
have two balls to go. If you run out of balls, you're out.
And at the end of the game, whoever has the most points
wins."

"What if there's a tie?" Max asked.

"Huh," said William, "not sure. Never happened. Does
everyone understand the rules?"

"Of course," said Max, who probably did. Tess wasn't
sure she understood, but she had a plan.

"Who wants to go first?" asked William. "Max?"

"No."

"Tess?"

"No. I want to go last." That was her plan. She figured
she'd get in a little learning time if she went last.

They each had their own tee stand, color-coded to
match their ball and their mallet. William set his into the
ground at the starting line about twenty feet from the gate.
He carefully placed his ball down on the center of it.

"Umpeer," he said.

Barnaby announced that the first hurdle would be
cleared when somebody hit the bell. "When ya ring the bell,
the gates'll open and we'll all move on to the second hole."

"Hit the rope cord, you mean?" asked Max.

"Something like that," said Barnaby, "although it's not quite that simple. Y'have to hit it in exactly the right place."

Barnaby smiled and put his face guard down.

"What's the face guard for?" asked Max.

Barnaby lifted it up to answer. "In case a ball goes haywire," he said. "You never know." He put his face guard down again.

Marie blew three notes into a flute, signifying that the game had begun.

the dangers of staring
directly at the moon

Definitely an unfair advantage," said Max to William. "I mean, you've played before. You know where the right place is."

This wasn't starting well.

Tess thought back to how it all began a week ago, when Max had thrown the Monopoly game at her. She wondered what the equivalent of throwing a Monopoly board was in miniature golf . . . ?

William gave Max a dirty look even though he had to admit it was true—he did have an unfair advantage.

But Tess smiled, as Max was doing exactly what she wanted—rattling William so hopefully his concentration was off and, in the process, probably rattling himself, as well.

William swung his mallet back and took a swing, stopping a half an inch away from the ball. He swung back again. And once again stopped his mallet a half an inch away from the ball. He swung his mallet again and hit the ball up too high, straight towards the top of the gate cord. He must've put some English on it as, just as it was about to hit, it made a slight right turn and dinged right into the gate itself. There was the most amazing noise when it hit—sort of metallic but a lot like a TV quiz show when someone gets the wrong answer. The noise seemed to echo across the moors, bouncing back and echoing again. Tess took it as a wake-up call. Focus.

Max was next. He placed his red ball on the tee. No hesitation, perfect swing, the crack of the ball going straight for the golden bell cord and hitting with precision right in the center. Weirdly, there was silence. No bells went off. The cord itself barely swayed.

"Foul!" cried Max, looking pleadingly at Barnaby.

Barnaby lifted his face mask up. "No. You have to hit it in exactly the right place."

Max puffed his cheeks out, which is what he did when he was frustrated. He reminded Tess of a little dog. Sometimes he'd scrape his foot on the ground, too, but he didn't do that this time.

"It's okay, Max. It's your first shot," said Marie. "And you hit exactly where you aimed. It was excellent." Tess loved the way Marie said *excellent*, her French accent sort of sneaked through. "You just don't know the trick yet."

Max nodded. He knew Marie was right. And he had hit it exactly where he'd aimed. He wondered if he'd hit it harder if it would've worked. But he hadn't lost his ball. Almost magically, it had rolled right back to him.

It was Tess's turn. She studied the castle gate intently. Something about the word *trick* had given her an idea. She remembered something she'd seen when they'd come in, the dark old-fashioned bell at the top of the rope cord. Impossible to see in miniature. *Or was it?* She reached down to her boot, as if she had an itch, and touched the skeleton key that was hiding there. She kept her eyes on the gate the whole time, studying every aspect of it. And just at the top, very faintly, at the top of the rope cord, was a tiny glimmer of gold that seemed to be in the shape of a miniature bell . . . Now, the trick was to actually hit it. She wondered if it was cheating . . . But her dad always said, "In games and in life, take advantage of what you have." Her dad hated to lose as much as she did. And as evidenced by Max's throwing of the Monopoly board a few days before, it might be something that ran in the family.

Her father had also taught her a bit about aim, as well. "The trick to aiming," he'd said, "is to keep your eye on the target. Yeah, yeah, you have to watch the ball. But imagine there's a line," he said, "between your eye, your shoulder, and your hand, and your eye is on the target. It works," he'd said. "It works much better than keeping your eye on the ball." And, Tess reasoned, at least she knew where the target was. Or, as her dad would say, "Advantage, Tess."

She took a practice swing, the way that William had, stopping her mallet about an inch away from the ball. Then she took another practice swing. She focused her eyes on the top of the rope cord. She swung again and hit a clear shot right to the gatepost, hitting the bottom of the bell exactly where she wanted. Sparks flew as the purple ball landed perfectly. And there was the sound of church-like bells, curiously accompanied by a distinctly punk rock drumbeat, as the gate flew wide open! Her ball bounced off the gate and landed on the other side, directly in front of the drawbridge! Score one for Tess.

"There's another rule I didn't tell you," said William. "Whoever clears a hurdle keeps their turn. You're still up, Tess."

They were at the drawbridge. This should be easy. It was just a straight shot across and up to the door of the castle.

"Pay attention, Missy," Barnaby mumbled under his face guard. But she didn't even hear him. She was feeling a little cocky. She swung and hit the ball perfectly. But as the ball started to cross the drawbridge, two silver fish, almost like dolphins, breached the water from the moat, as if they were going to kiss in mid-air, and one of them swallowed her ball.

"That's not fair," said Tess.

Barnaby lifted his face guard up. "I tried to warn ya, Missy, but you were feelin' a little overconfident.

"One point for Tess. And one ball down for Tess," said Barnaby in his best official umpire voice. He ceremoniously handed her a replacement ball. And then, as if he were making an announcement to a crowd, "Lord William's up," he said, "and not quite on the green." Barnaby put his face guard down again.

"Are you a lord?" asked Tess.

"Not quite, I think, but I will be some day," said William.

A Lord and a Third, thought Tess. *Wow.* She and Max exchanged a look. Tess wondered if they were playing out of their league.

Tess knew William would make this next point. He knew this course like the back of his hand. And, if there were any timing to the jumping of the shimmery silver fish, for sure he had it down. She folded her arms and stood on the sidelines. Sure enough, he cleared it in one shot, straight across the drawbridge and right up to the front door, where it careened against the family crest and opened that as well.

"Oh my goodness," said Barnaby, emerging from his face mask again. "I guess we'd call that a two-fer."

Both Tess and Max were feeling out-gamed. It's not that much fun to compete if you don't have a chance.

But William's ball had landed in a very inconvenient place, right up against a miniature table leg and next to a wall. There was no way to swing the mallet and get a clean shot.

Barnaby lifted his face mask up. "House rules, William. No skipping turns and you have to hit your own ball, even if there's no way to make a real shot."

Max felt encouraged. Maybe there was a chance after all. William had to hit his ball so it would probably
bounce off the wall and, odds were, land somewhere
more hittable, so to speak. William had to practically
turn himself into a pretzel to get his mallet close enough
to the ball and tap it. And sure enough, it bounced off the
wall and rolled onto the miniature antique carpet, leaving
a potential clear shot for Max out the back door to the
miniature backyard, or, as they referred to it in this game,
the green.

Max was up. Carefully, he set his red ball on the tee on
the miniature carpet in exactly the place where William's
had been. He had a chance to at least score. It was a straight
shot out the back door. How hard could that be?

No problem, except he over-estimated his strength
and went right off the green and onto the lawn of the
backyard. He looked over at the umpeer to see what that
meant . . .

"You're not out, M'boy. Y'get one shot to hit it back
on the green."

But just as Barnaby said it, the sky started to darken
above them. It was the most curious thing. And all of
them looked up and stared at the moon. It was that rarest
of events. An eclipse, when the earth passes between the

sun and the moon and over the course of an hour or so, the moon will darken and appear red, blood-red, a red moon, but even rarer still, on the occasion of a blue moon, the second full moon in a month. Was there a prophecy to it? If there was, no one had told them. But the night sky darkened as the eclipse was starting . . .

Max was mesmerized by it. He took a step back on the lawn and then another and then a few more to get a better view. Tess looked over and screamed as Max stepped into the hawthorn trees and . . . simply disappeared.

the other side of the hawthorn trees

What struck Max first was the silence, the absolute, total, and complete silence. There were no night sounds, no crickets, not even a lone bird chirping, no voices. He'd never heard true silence before. It was all-encompassing. It was very lonely. Max wondered—because he was Max and he wondered things like this—if this was what infinity was. There was no sign of anyone, no movement. He realized he'd never been so alone before.

The moon was red now, the eclipse in full swing, and it shined on the ground—he noticed the ground, the absolute desolate ground—making the dirt appear, also, almost orange, red, then a darker red. It wasn't even ground. It was rocks or something like that. There were no stars visible in the sky. It was just the perfect circle of the blood-red moon. At first.

He must've hit his head. It was the only thing he could think of.

He must've hit his head and he hoped he'd come to soon. He'd never knocked himself out before. That must be what it was.

"Help me," Max cried out. His words seem to echo across the rocks in the otherwise silent landscape. He wondered if anyone could hear him.

*if only there was
one last wish...*

Tess held her breath. Any moment now, Max would reappear. He'd pop out of the hawthorn trees, a scratch on his face, that funny grin, holding the miniature golf ball up like a trophy. But there wasn't even a trace of where he'd disappeared, as if the hedge had simply closed up behind him. She counted to ten. Not true, she only got to three, and then began running toward the hawthorn trees herself.

She felt two arms around her, like a vise, holding her. "No, no, no, Tess. Y'can't go into the hawthorn."

She looked up at Barnaby. "But—" she was sobbing now, "but I have to go after him. I can't—I can't lose Max!"

As she said it, out of the corner of her eye she saw William run, faster almost than she'd seen anyone ever run before, straight into the hawthorn. And he, too, simply disappeared.

Marie turned pale. Barnaby gasped, emitting a sigh so loud it seemed to echo. The sky was dark now. Not even stars. Just the spectre of the red moon as the eclipse neared its peak.

Tess held her breath again and waited. Surely, William would come back through the hawthorn any moment, pushing Max in front of him. But instead there was nothing. Not even a sound from the other side of the hedge. A strange quiet had settled over the garden and it was as if the hawthorn trees had knitted up and closed behind William, as well, as if no one had gone through them at all.

Something else was happening, too. A strange mist was settling over the castle and the gardens. Tess couldn't tell if it was coming from the air or the ground.

Everything seemed to be fading. The roses, the pond, the frogs themselves seemed to be losing their color. It happened so quickly, and then it seemed to be happening in slow motion, or slow-motion capture, staggered, as if time itself were slowing down, as the colors faded. The grass was paler. The castle itself seemed to be losing its corners, its edges, as if it were being swallowed by the mist.

Marie had fallen to the ground, her head resting on the pale grass, appearing as if she was so weak she couldn't lift herself.

"I have to try to save them," Tess said to Barnaby. "I have to at least try. There isn't any choice. I have to. I have to find them." She was shaking now but with a kind of strength not fear. "I have to try to save all of us. If I can . . ." Somehow she knew that the things were connected, or she hoped they were anyway, Max and William disappearing through the hedgerow, the spectre of the moon, the castle that seemed to be disappearing in the mist.

She wrenched herself out of Barnaby's arms and began running across the lawn, the stalks of which were almost white. She barely heard the sound of her own feet as they hit the ground, as if sound were fading, too. She could hear the sound of her own heartbeat though, as if it were keeping time, as if it were urging her to hurry.

She ran toward the sculpture garden. Once there, she was struck by how gray it was, as if the shining white marble had faded to stone, as if they were ruins, built hundreds of years ago, shattered by time, the marble structures crumbling, the faces of the statues partly worn away. She barely stopped to touch the cool white marble of Athena as she passed and almost cut herself on what was now rough stone . . . She looked up at Athena and empty eyes stared back at her, vacant where the sapphires had been only an hour before. Poseidon's crown was cracked and his trident was missing prongs, as if it could no longer find its way or lead a traveller on theirs. She wondered if she should stop and kneel. But there was no time to pray.

She ran on, up the hill, and to the carousel. But where the merry-go-round had been, there was just a bare patch of ground. It wasn't making any sense to Tess. She thought she must've run the wrong direction. But then she saw a square concrete slab on the ground that seemed to be exactly where the turnstile had been and another larger round concrete slab where the merry-go-round might have been. *Had she run in the wrong direction?* But no, the canopy was there, as if it had once housed a carousel.

She said it out loud, not that there was anyone who could hear it.

"I have to have another wish. I have to," she said.

She shut her eyes and reached her hand down into her boot and touched the skeleton key and made a wish. Silently, so she was sure that no one could hear it. It had to be particularly worded. It had to be a wish, just one, but a wish for all of them.

She opened her eyes. And then she heard something above her on the hill, the faintest sound, as if a door was slamming in the wind, and a strange grating sound, like wheels grinding on dirt. She looked and saw a wood shack that seemed as if it might be a stable. She ran towards it.

There was an old wood-framed barn, white-washed, or maybe just the color had faded from it, too. The stable door was almost falling off its top hinge so that it scraped across the ground and almost fell as she pulled it open. She entered cautiously. The wood planks were practically rotten, littered with wet straw. There were four stalls. There was a tin bucket, rusted, empty except for one apple that was more than a week old. She took the apple, hoping it, too, wouldn't crumble in her hand, and started to walk through the barn, testing out each step tentatively, in case the wood was rotted straight through. The first stall was empty, the stall directly across from it was missing its back wall so it looked right out onto the pale gray landscape. In the next stall there was just a bale of hay so dry it looked like a bamboo box. The stall across from it was empty. Tess heard the sound of hooves in a back stall pounding madly at the dirt. She ran to it. There was a large black stallion saddled as if he were waiting for her to arrive. He seemed so angry, as if his eyes were, also, flashing sparks or else something was spooking him. She heard the wheels of a carriage pulling in at the back. She didn't wait to see who that was. There was no time. The ground beneath her feet was almost white like sand.

She opened the stall and the stallion went to kick her. Right hoof to her jaw. She ducked. She stood again and tried to stare him down. She put her hand on the horse's nose to try to calm him, but he shook her off. She held the apple up. He shook his head as he bit it from her hand, but it seemed to quiet him. She shut her eyes again and made the wish.

She put her foot in the stirrup and hoisted herself onto the saddle, but he was almost too big for her, she lost her footing, and then she felt hands around her waist lifting her up . . .

She looked behind her. There was an elegant gentleman in old-fashioned riding clothes, with high cheekbones and the darkest hair, a black cape around his shoulders, and eyes that somehow reminded her of William's. "Please, dear," he said, "bring M'boy back to me." The gentleman nodded and Tess nodded back.

Before she could even properly grip the reins or lead him out of the stable, the stallion took off, almost crushing Tess's leg as he careened into the stall on the other side of the stable. He was nearly impossible to control. Her right index finger was barely holding the rough leather reins, her left hand was gripping the back of the saddle to try to hold her seat. She hugged him tightly with her legs, mostly to keep her mount, but also to remind him that she was there. She leaned in and whispered, "I am your Lady and you are my Knight. And we can *only* do this together." The horse didn't respond at all. He continued to race with no regard for the fact that she was on his back. The horse raced so quickly, he left a cloud of his own dust behind him.

She held the reins tightly now in her right hand, trying to guide him, without too much success. As they tore at record speed through the sculpture garden, they almost crashed into the fountain and Poseidon's spear. She heard the sound of rocks breaking as if the sculptures were crumbling into ruins around them. She wondered what would happen if Poseidon were to drop his spear—would all travellers lose their way?

She wished she was imagining things. Whatever was going on was real, stark, dangerous, and she and the horse seemed to be the only ones with two whits of sense about them and any semblance of strength and direction.

The black stallion raced on to the garden with no concern that she was seated on his back, heading at breakneck speed toward the hedge of hawthorn, like a foxhound who had hold of a scent. No, that wasn't the way it could happen. She knew that. And then she realized what wasn't right; she hadn't stated it correctly. She leaned in again, gripping him tightly with her thighs, her face up next to his, her mouth right by his ear. "I am your Knight and you are my Steed," she whispered in a much stronger tone of voice, "and together we will succeed."

Tess pulled back on the reins. She pulled again. She whispered in his ear again. "Halt! You have to let me be the guide. But first I'm going to name you. I call you Midnight and you will follow my command." She pulled back on the reins again. Then, did it one more time. "Whoa! Midnight! You *are* my horse and you will do as I say."

Midnight seemed to understand each word she said and came to a complete stop less than three inches away from the hedge of hawthorn trees, so abruptly that Tess was almost thrown head first from the saddle. Her back hurt as if her spine had been twisted and she had whiplash already from the ride. She kept her shoulders up, her head erect, her right hand firmly on the reins, as she gently and firmly turned Midnight around. "Good boy. That's good. We can do this if we do it together." He was obeying her commands now. "We have to do this together," she whispered again in his ear.

Marie and Barnaby were both standing now on the lawn, Marie so pale, she looked as if she might be fading, too. The landscape around them in the garden seemed to have changed from a watercolor to an almost black-and-white photo with a sepia tone.

As Tess led Midnight directly back towards the castle, she noticed his gait was almost that of a military horse, each hoofbeat as if it were marching to a silent drum. The castle itself was almost completely hidden by the mist. She wondered if it was hidden or if it was disappearing, too? The moon was still red in the sky above her, a red circle against an almost black sky.

She turned Midnight around again with a firm hand

on the reins, pushing his neck ever so slightly with her other hand, stroking his mane as she did it, until both of their backs were to the castle and she had a clear view looking out over the lawn, directly facing the thick hedge of hawthorn trees like an ominous wall at the edge of the garden . . .

She tried to calculate the distance. There was no time to start slowly and gather speed. They had to start at racetrack speed. She leaned in and whispered again in his ear. She hit his sides softly but firmly with her heels. He knew. He sensed it. As if he were a racehorse trained for winning and the gates had just come up, Midnight broke into a gallop and then performed the most extraordinary jump, almost like an arc in the sky, blue medal for sure.

But as they started to land on the other side, Tess turned her head to see if she could catch sight of Max or William—nothing, just red desolate rock. She turned her head again and lost her balance as if she were going in a different trajectory than the straight and steady course of the black stallion Midnight . . . and she was thrown from his back.

She landed on the harsh, desolate ground. She felt the rocks slice into her left side almost like razors or the sharp edges of swords. As the side of her head hit the jagged ground, as if a curtain fell, all she saw was blackness.

the terrible morphons and the strange sky

T ess . . . Tess . . . !"

She could hear Max's voice in the distance, oddly amplified, as if it were coming through a wind tunnel.

She opened her eyes. Blurry, at first, and then the sky came into sharp focus. It wasn't like any night sky she'd ever seen before.

Was she seeing double, were there two moons? No,

just a large red sphere that looked like Jupiter and, just below it, a bright light sphere with rings that looked like Saturn. Directly at eye level, quite low as she was still lying down, the full blood moon, its bottom almost at the line of the horizon. The sky itself was so peculiar—not at all like the night sky we are accustomed to. Mars, the red planet, just above. But there were no stars. It seemed to have no view of anything but our own solar system.

Tess felt a sharp pain in her upper arm and another in her back and in her right ankle. She felt a throbbing pain in her temple or was it in the back of her head, she couldn't tell. She did not know how long she'd lain there. She felt cold, then hot, as if the rocks were the temperature of dry ice.

She heard Max's voice again, almost as if it were an echo, "Tess, Tess, Tess, are you all right?" She saw him leaning over her.

Max . . . she went to speak, but no words came out.

She felt his hand on her forehead. Everything was spinning a bit until it came into a red-hazed focus, as if someone had laid a filter the color of blazing ash across the air.

"Where do you think we are?" asked Max, hardly hiding the fear in his voice.

"On the other side of the hawthorn," she answered.

"See," she said, "now I'm the one who's being logical." Her dad had taught them: "If you're really terrified, try to make a joke and put the other person at ease. Calm minds have a better chance of solving things."

But then Tess looked up at the unfamiliar sky. "What do you think of the sky, Max?" she asked, sounding more terrified than he had.

"It's not like any sky I've ever seen," he answered. "If I didn't know better, I'd say we were in space, having a closed view of our own solar system."

"That's what I thought, too. But I don't know what that means." In a way she was relieved that Max saw it, too. Although, it occurred to her that maybe she shouldn't have been . . .

And then William had his hands gently on her shoulders, as well. Tess wondered if she was having trouble seeing. He looked so pale, so faint, as if he, too, was covered in mist. His voice was almost a whisper. "I thought I was never going to see you again," he said. She felt his hand gently stroke her forehead.

Her eyes started to close, as if she was going to pass out again. She forced herself to open her eyes. She flexed her legs. She made a fist with her free left hand and gripped William's tighter with the other. There was something about the way the moon was dropping in the sky that frightened her. She worried that there wasn't any time.

She heard the black stallion, Midnight, and turned to see him standing at attention. His coat was matted with sweat and his eyes were fierce, but he was upright. She had been so frightened he had fallen, too.

Max could sense her thought. "He only stumbled. It was you that fell. Tess, are you all right?"

There wasn't any choice but to be all right. The moon was still dropping toward the horizon, as if it would soon set the way that the sun does. "Pull me up, Max. William, keep holding my other hand."

It took all of Max's strength to pull her to a standing position—he wasn't sure he was getting any help from William, who seemed to have no strength left at all. Tess stood steady on her feet even though the images around her were still a little blurry.

Now the ground beneath them was doing something strange, as well. The rocks were bleeding rivulets of red sand. There were tiny geysers, as if the earth itself was bubbling, the way a volcano does before it starts to erupt. There were large plumes of steam coming up from between the rocks. And it was as if the rocks themselves were melting and erupting up from the ground, morphing, turning into creatures—or what Tess imagined were creatures—a gryphon? She couldn't remember what a gryphon was, but then the image changed to something like a lizard that opened its large, triangular jaw, or was it an alligator with the body of a bear? Tess pulled Max away from the hot breath of the imagined creature. *Or were they imagined?*

"The Morphons," William said unprompted. "Don't look at them. Be careful not to look at them."

There was something with the neck of a giraffe with a body that looked like the shell of a snail. The thin body of a fawn with the large shoulders and trunk of an elephant, and then it changed into the royal head of a lion . . . the images were confused, distorted. Nothing about the creatures was constant and yet Tess felt that any moment, they could band together, turn into a herd, and simply . . .

"Just look at each other," William said. "Just look . . ." His voice got fainter.

"Max, help me with William."

"I'm not sure he's the only one who needs help," said Max.

"We'll worry about me later," said Tess. William was so pale. He looked as if he could barely stand. They lifted him between them and put his foot in the stirrup. Max had to lift and push William's leg over the saddle to the other side, as if he was a doll, and run around to catch him, as he was, then, quite in danger of falling over.

Max jumped up onto the horse behind William and wrapped his arms around William's waist.

Tess put her foot in the stirrup, but something pulled her back to the ground, something that didn't feel like gravity, at all.

She put her foot back in the stirrup and, with all the strength she had, pulled herself up, hoisted herself on the horse in front of William and Max. "Hold on to me, William." She felt his weak hands clasp around her waist. She reached down and touched his hand, it was so cold.

The creatures below in the ground seemed to be grabbing up for them, trying to catch a hold of their legs and feet or, more frightening still, catch them in a stare.

"Don't look," said William, his voice barely a whisper. There were faces now below them in the rocks, the creatures all had faces. "Don't look. If you look at them, they'll try to steal your soul." Tess didn't even want to think about what that meant. But Max was mesmerized.

Tess turned and saw him staring at a creature that, at first, looked like a seal and then morphed into something more human-like. There was fire in its eyes, its jaw started to define itself, and limbs appeared with claw-like hands. Its features started to resemble Max's.

"You'll forgive me for this, one day," said Tess, and she reached around William and slapped Max straight across the face as hard as she could to try to break his stare. "I'm sorry, Max, I'm sorry," she said as Max snapped out of it and held his hand up to his cheek.

Tess heard her father's voice in her head. *If you get lost . . . try to get back to where you started, if you can . . .*

She leaned in and took hold of the reins. She whispered in the horse's ear, "Don't think about it. You simply have to run. Run and then jump."

Like a cold bath of ice, the air hit them as they started to race forward. William whispering to all of them, "Don't look down."

Beneath the horses' hooves, the rocks were pulverizing, turning into sand, red sand, but sand with a hot breath that seemed to lap at their heels . . . and morph, morph into creatures that wanted their very breath.

"Pretend it's a desert," she whispered in the horse's ear again. "You can do that, can't you? That we're somewhere on the Arabian Peninsula where your grandfather used to run . . . run, Midnight, run. Hold on to me, Max, hold to William."

She reached down to touch the key in her boot. She shut her eyes and made a wish, silently, to herself. It was the same wish she'd made before in the abandoned merry-go-round shell. *Please, please, bring us all home safely and let us be reunited with the ones we love. That's my wish. That's always been my wish.*

trying to get back to where they started...

It felt as if there was a blast of hot air behind them, chasing them, trying to sweep them up, swallow them, in its heat. Tess turned and saw what looked like the shape of a dragon, or was it a dinosaur shooting fire from its jaws? *Don't look at it. Don't look at it. Don't let its eyes grab yours.* She turned away and kicked Midnight sharply with her heels.

The only sightline was the wall of mist directly in

front of them, impossible to see through, like a wall of fog. They were gaining speed as Midnight raced toward what appeared to be nothingness—*nothingness nothingness nothingness*—a bit like the invisible wall Tess had encountered when she'd first tried to enter the garden. She wanted to stop but the roar of the creature behind them indicated it was clearly gaining speed. As they hurtled forward at breakneck speed, Tess hoped that, somewhere there, it was really the back-side of the hedge of hawthorn trees, even though they couldn't see it. And that Midnight would sense that it was there.

If you get lost, try to get back to where you started.

Midnight jumped, almost as if he were sailing into the air. It went on for the longest time, as if they were moving again in slow motion, or time capture, or something odd, that didn't have to do with the way time usually worked. It was as if Tess could see and feel each frame of their movement and then time sped up again, or was it just her heart that was racing, as she felt them descend and land and the stallion continued running. Everything was a blur around them, a fog of mist so heavy that it was all that she could see.

She shut her eyes for a moment, and when she opened them, the fog seemed to be swirling in a kaleidoscope of color, catching the rays of the moon, which was white now, white and full, like the night sky when it was normal. She heard Marie laugh, that laugh that sounded like a bell, and nothing had ever sounded so pure or reassuring before. She felt arms around her and heard Barnaby's voice. "You're safe now, M'Lady," he said as he lifted her down from the horse. Max was beside her, holding on to her waist, his head on her shoulder, as if he'd quite reverted to being a little boy. And there was William being held so closely by Marie. All the color had returned to both of their faces.

Marie was laughing and there were tears streaming down her face. Their mother did that sometimes, too—laughed so hard at something one of them did that she would cry. But in this case, Tess didn't know if the laughter came before the tears or if it was the other way around.

The gentleman who'd helped her at the stable was standing next to Marie and William. He looked strong and elegant and noble. And he was hugging both Marie and William.

William was holding on to him, too. "Papa, you're home," he said. "I didn't know if you were ever coming home."

The gentleman smiled and said softly, "I could say the same thing about you."

Tess realized it was William's father and that he *had* finally come home. She realized she was crying, but they were tears of joy and relief.

She couldn't help but wonder how Marie fit in. There was something odd about the way they were holding one another. There was more than affection for Marie in William's father's eyes.

"Papa, you've finally come home," William said again. He was still holding on to his father as if he never wanted to let go.

Tess realized she would probably feel the same way if she could see her father right now.

Barnaby was tending the horse's right hoof, which was cut and bleeding. "Is Midnight okay?" Tess asked.

"Midnight, huh? I see you've named him, then. Ornery stallion but admirable. His leg's not broken, at least," said Barnaby, "which I regard as something of a miracle. His hooves are charred, though. The whole lot of you's lucky, if you ask me."

"I don't think anything's broken," said Tess. "Although I still do have a bit of a headache."

She realized William was introducing her to his father. "Yes, Sir, pleased to meet you," she managed as she extended her right hand out to his.

"We met for a moment," he said, "at the stable, but we didn't have time for proper hellos. Have you always been so brave?" he asked her.

"My father would say," she answered truthfully, "that I don't think long enough to be afraid. I just act instantly."

William's father laughed but then added, "Well, I would say, you're very brave. And I would also say, 'thank you'."

Tess wanted to explain that she hadn't been brave at all, that it had been instinct—she couldn't lose Max or William.

"It's terribly late," said Barnaby. "I'm surprised that your aunt hasn't come after you yet . . . She could be half hysterical."

"Her name is Evie," said Max.

"I know her name," said Barnaby. "I just hope she still wants to know mine. I'll take you home right now," he said.

Tess stopped to hug Marie, who whispered in her ear, "Always be the way you are, dear. Always be the way you are." It was just a half whisper but her voice was as clear as if she were speaking through a microphone. There was something odd about it, as if it was the sort of thing one would say if they weren't going to see you again or were sending you off on a journey. Tess knew they were words she would always remember, as she would remember every moment of that night, as if it were etched in glass.

Her memory would include the moment when William took her hand as they were walking through the house to the big front door that led to the drawbridge. As he was about to open the door, he said, "Wait, wait here," and ran up the big flight of stairs.

Max had already gone outside. Tess waited. She took one last look into the dining room. The lights had been dimmed and everything appeared completely normal. William came back down the stairs, holding something carefully in his arms. It was the antique porcelain doll that he told her his grandfather had given to him and that had been his mother's. "I want you to have it," he said.

Tess shook her head. "I couldn't take it," she said. "It wouldn't be right—it was your mom's."

"No," he insisted, "it would be right. I think she would want you to have it, too." He'd affixed the doll to the wooden base. "You remember how it works, don't you? Just wind it up . . ."

She held the doll carefully in her arms. It was extraordinary how life-like and delicate the face was, each strand of its hair so carefully framed around the face, the eyelashes seemed almost to be real. "I'll take good care of her," said Tess. "Thank you."

Barnaby had brought the buggy around and two ginger-colored horses were harnessed to it, looking quite frisky and ready to go. They had bells around their necks so people would know they were coming in the darkness. "Midnight's resting," he said to Tess, as if he anticipated her question.

And then William hugged her, and she felt his lips slightly graze her neck as he whispered in her ear. "Keep the key," he said, "you never know when you might need it."

sometimes wishes do come true

Should I come in, M'Lady, and try to explain?" Barnaby asked Tess when they pulled up and saw Aunt Evie's Bentley parked in the driveway.

Max answered him immediately, "Oh, no. That would only make things worse."

"Seeing as how she sees *you* as a responsible adult," Tess explained, "she'd probably yell at you. She won't be mad at us," Tess added. "She'll just be glad we're home."

Aunt Evie hadn't even noticed that the children weren't home. She had only just arrived herself. She'd assumed they were upstairs sleeping in their beds.

Tess and Max tiptoed in the front door so as not to wake Aunt Evie, who they assumed might be asleep in her bed. Tess set the doll on the front table and they heard noises in the kitchen.

Aunt Evie had *not* gone to play poker at the White Horse. She'd had her own version of an adventure involving the train station and what would be a very big surprise for the children.

"I think we should wake them up," a man's voice said. It sounded so familiar, booming through the house. The kind of voice that tends to narrate things, give one reassurance, speak in declarative sentences, as if he is quite certain about everything he says.

"Daddy!" Tess screamed. She'd recognize his voice anywhere. "Daddy . . ."

She and Max both raced toward the kitchen. And there he was, looking somewhat thinner than the last time they'd seen him. His face was tanned from the desert sun. At the first glimpse of them, he broke into a smile, that smile he had that wasn't like anyone else's. Tess threw her arms around him and threw herself into his lap, the way she used to when she was little. Max went right behind him and wrapped his arms around his father's neck, throwing his head onto his father's shoulder as he did it. And they were together again. He was home. He was safe. Tess's wishes had come true. She realized her wish had come true for William, too.

Their father had a sat phone. That was short for *satellite*, and it worked anywhere, even when there wasn't local cell service. They immediately turned the Skype feature on and called their mom in New York. They all crowded into the tiny screen, Tess, Max, their dad, and Aunt Evie. "Hello," they shouted, pretending they were calling from outer space.

"I love you, Mommy," said Tess, all of her toughness disappearing in that moment.

It was only Aunt Evie who noticed that her sister looked awfully thin and pale.

"Dad's fine," said Tess before their mother could ask anything.

Their mother laughed, "I was about to ask him about you two."

"We're fine," said Tess.

"We are," said Max, "we even talk to each other sometimes now." Their mother laughed again, which confused Max, who was so literal, he didn't realize he'd said something funny.

"We'll see you in two days," their father said. "I love you."

the curious story of
the castle in the mist

Sunday was a blur of laughter, packing, dinosaur pancakes (their dad's specialty), and trying to persuade Aunt Evie to come back to the States with them and spend a few weeks at their house on Long Island. Aunt Evie agreed to come but not until the end of August. It was only the first of July.

Neither Max nor Tess could stop smiling. They were going home. And, on top of that, they weren't going back to boarding school in September, which Tess was equally thrilled about. She and Max were going to go back to the Country Day School in Greenwich Village—the little school they'd gone to since kindergarten with the friends they'd had since they were little and their mother always just a few blocks away. For the first time, Tess truly understood why being happy was something that could make you cry.

On Monday morning at 9:00 A.M., there was a knock at Aunt Evie's door. A driver in a uniform and cap was at the door and a sedate black sedan was parked at the curb. The network had sent him to drive them to Heathrow Airport.

They couldn't thank Aunt Evie enough. Even Max threw his arms around her neck and kissed her cheek. Aunt Evie suddenly realized how quiet the house was going to be without them, which was both the good news and the bad.

"G'wan," she said, "g'wan. Get outta here. I'll see you both in a couple of weeks."

When the door shut to the car and the driver started the engine, Tess asked if they could just run up the road and say good-bye to William. "Could we, Daddy? Please. Is there time? He won't understand what's happened to us if we don't say good-bye."

"Is there time?" their father asked the driver.

"Yes, Sir. Quite a bit of time, it only takes two hours

and you have five hours before your plane. I assumed you might want to stop for a sandwich, one last cup of tea."

"That, too, if there's time," said their father. "But do you know where it is, Tess?"

"Yes, of course I do. Can you just drive up the road? How far do you think it is, Max?"

"Not more than a mile, I don't think."

It was more than a mile, although in England they called them kilometers. It was almost three miles (or rather, 4.8 kilometers) up the road and Tess thought for a moment, perhaps, they'd driven the wrong direction. But then they saw the gates that enclosed the castle and the unmistakable planks of the drawbridge.

Tess almost squealed. "Come on, Dad. Come with us. They'll want to meet you, too!"

She scrambled out of the car and went to ring the bell, but something stopped her. "Look, Max."

There was a plaque by the gate:

BRAMSFIELD CASTLE

MUSEUM HOURS:
Tuesday—Saturday
10 A.M.—6 P.M.

Once in a blue moon—open till midnight

"That's an odd sign," their father said instantly. "Do you think that means they sometimes rent it out for parties?" Tess and Max exchanged a look.

Tess was a little confused, as she hadn't realized it was a museum.

"In any event," their dad added, "it's Monday, so they're closed."

"Well, they'll still be there, Papa," said Tess. "I mean, they live here."

She pulled on the bell cord. She looked through the gate and saw the silver fish shimmering in the water underneath the drawbridge.

After the longest time, nobody came. Tess pulled on the cord again. And so did Max.

"Maybe they've gone out," their father suggested.

"No," said Tess. "They don't really go out very much." She pulled on the cord again, even though she knew it was bordering on rude.

"Hold yer horses," they heard a voice calling. The thick Irish accent sounded awfully familiar.

The gentleman who opened the door was older than Barnaby. He was a few inches shorter, too. He had a shock of white hair that was visible under the herringbone cap he wore (that looked a lot like the herringbone cap that Barnaby wore).

"We were starting to think no one was here," their dad said in his loud and booming voice. "Thanks for opening the door."

"Americans," the gentleman said, in a thick Irish brogue. "Museum's closed on Monday. How long will you be in town?"

"I'm afraid we're leaving today," their father answered.

"Really?" he replied. "Hmmm, seeing as you're leaving today, I suppose I could break the rules and let you in. It won't be an official tour, but at least you'll get to see the place."

"We wanted to see William," Tess added.

"William? And what William would that be, M'Lady?"

The *M'Lady* stopped her.

"Umm," she looked at Max and then back at the museum guard, "a-a," she almost stammered, "a young boy about our age. William. We thought this was his house."

But the museum guard had walked ahead of them, briskly crossing the drawbridge toward the castle, and seemingly wasn't paying attention to anything she said.

They followed him across the drawbridge and into the house.

Tess took a breath as she looked around. It was the same furniture that had been there before, the same staircase, the view into the dining room was just the same, except that there was a velvet rope enclosing the table and chairs so that no one would or could sit on them. The crystal prisms seemed to still be hanging in the window, refracting the light and making criss-cross rainbow patterns on the dining room floor.

Tess repeated, "We were—we were looking for William."

"Nobody lives here," the museum guard explained. "No one but me, and I live out in a small house by the stable."

Tess knew where the stable was, but she didn't say anything.

"Nobody's lived here for almost fifty years," the museum guard explained. "We're thinking we should have a party for the bicentennial."

Tess wondered what that celebration would be like . . .

"It's a curious story," he said. "But I suppose y'don't have time for it . . ."

Tess and Max looked at their father.

"Could you tell the abbreviated version?" their father boomed, his voice sounding louder in the castle than it ever had anywhere, as if it were echoing through the halls.

"It was war time," said Barnaby. "The First World

War. The young lord was a decorated soldier and he was sent to France. He fell in love with a beautiful French girl with no parentage at all. She'd been left on a church step and raised by nuns. She had no known history. The young lord believed his father would approve—if he just met her, he would see. But the old earl, enraged, cut him off before he could even bring his young bride home. He disinherited him, sent a courier to tell him never to come home. Shortly after that, the young lord disappeared in battle. Do you know what that means?" he asked the children. "'Disappeared in battle'?"

Tess and Max nodded. They both knew, too well, what it meant to disappear in battle. They lived with the fear of it almost every day. Especially when their father was reporting from the battlefield, embedded with the troops. But right now, he was right there, by their side, and there wasn't anything to be afraid of. Tess slipped her hand into her father's and held on tightly as she and Max nodded again and the museum guard continued to explain.

"The Royal Guards came and told him. One day they rang the bell and walked across the drawbridge.

"'We're so sorry, M'Lord,' they said, 'your son has been lost in battle.

"'No, we can't confirm his death, just that he's among the missing.'

"It was a few months later," he went on, "that there was another ring of the bell and a young, waifish woman with a young boy in her arms appeared at the castle door. She told 'im she was a governess. That's what she told 'im and he believed her, why would he not? She knew if she told him the truth, he'd turn her away. She told him she was the governess and that she carried his four-year-old grandson in her arms. She told him that both his son and his son's wife, the child's mother, had disappeared and that they'd told her when she first came to work for them, that if anything ever happened to them, she should come here.

"She set the boy down. He was the spitting image of his father, dressed in a blue suit of the day with short pants, an elegant air about him, and an impish smile, although if anyone had looked closely, they might've noticed that the blue pants were the same color as the cotton the peasants often wore in France and the suit was hand sewn. But there was no question, he was the young lord. No one could question that. He put his hand out to his grandfather and said, in a perfect English accent, 'Pleased to meet you, Sir,' as if he were a much older boy than he was. And he melted the old man's heart.

"The governess produced a sealed envelope. 'Your son said I was to give this to you,' she said and handed the old Lord a letter that had been sealed with the family crest.

> Dear Father,
>
> If you are receiving this letter something has happened to me and to Sophie. And I trust the bearer Marie Duchamp to bring you our son. It is my hope and wish that you will take him in and raise him as your own. And also, as your own health has been somewhat fragile, it is my wish that you will retain Marie and that you might make arrangements for her and William to live on at home, at the castle, with William under her care until he comes of age were anything to happen to you. Yes, we named him William. William III.

"'If I may, Sir,' the governess went on, 'it was their wish, if you were to take the boy in, that I might be allowed to stay on. I was a teacher at the American School in Alsace before your son and his wife hired me—I know you probably don't think much of Americans or American education or French women, for that matter. For the record, I am French, but I was schooled in Switzerland.'

"She was lying, of course, not about the fact that she was French. She was not the boy's governess. She was his mother. She was his son's wife. She was the old Earl's daughter-in-law. But she knew, if she told him the truth, he would send her away.

"The old Earl looked back to the letter, which went on:

I had always hoped we would be reconciled and that you would know and love my wife, Sophie, as I do. But I know that you will not be able to turn your grandson away. He looks so much like the portrait of you when you were a boy, Papa, that I sometimes expect him to sound like you, too.

If you do receive this letter and all is not lost, that we have only been detained or separated by the winds of war,

Sophie and I have made a solemn promise that somehow, somehow, we will make our way back to the castle and be reunited, even if it takes a blue moon.

with admiration, respect, and love,

your son,

William II "

The letter was framed in a glass case on display in the hallway. The handwriting clear and ornate, the crest visible at the top of the paper. Tess lingered and read the letter herself. She said out loud, "Even if it takes a blue moon . . ."

Max started to say something . . . but Tess silenced him with a look as the museum guard led them into the garden and went on with his narration. "To the old Earl," he continued, "the boy looked so much like his son that there was no way he could send him away."

They were out in the garden now. Tess could see the line of hawthorn trees forming a hedge on the other side of the garden. She and Max instinctively linked pinkies as they walked.

"The grounds are beautifully kept," their father said.

"Yes," said the guard, "there's even a maze up there."

Tess realized that was one of the places they hadn't been, the maze, and wondered what dangers possibly lurked there.

"At first, the old Earl didn't have much to do with his grandson, but eventually the two became inseparable. They would go for a horse ride most mornings, no matter how rainy the weather was. And on the boy's eighth birthday, he shipped in a carousel from France."

"A carousel?" said Tess inquisitively. "A merry-go-round? A real one?" She couldn't help it that there was an edge in her voice. The museum guard sounded so much like Barnaby that she was trying to figure how he could be three inches shorter than he was last night. Or why he would be telling a story like this, treating them like tourists, when it was so clear that they knew each other.

"Could we see the merry-go-round?" The questions came on top of each other. "Is there time, Dad? Is it still here, Sir?" She didn't know how to address the guard, so she called him Sir. She was overexcited now. She wanted something to make sense or to find something she could touch that would somehow make her understand. Or believe, believe she hadn't imagined it all. But how could she have?

"Yes, it's still here. Afraid it doesn't work any more. But y'can see it if you like, if your father says there's time."

"There's time," their father said, "if we hurry."

The museum guard started to walk quickly across the lawn, their father quite in step with him, Max and Tess hurrying behind.

"Do you ever rent it out?" asked Max. "Like a hotel? Where you let people spend the night? Do you ever rent it out for parties? Weddings. It would be a great place for a wedding. Don't you think, Tess?"

"Practically storybook," said Tess with even more of an edge in her voice. Merry-go-round, indeed, of course there was. *Did he think they were foolish?*

"Oh Lord, no. It's never rented," the museum guard replied. "The place has been left with clear instructions that *everything* is to be left as it is, forever, undisturbed, preserved, that everything is to be exactly where it was left, even the toys in young William's bedroom, even the carousel."

They were walking through the sculpture garden now.

Their father stopped in front of the fountain with the statue of Poseidon holding the sceptre in his right hand.

"This *is* like a museum," their father remarked, "somewhere you might wander into in Florence." He turned his attention to the extraordinary white alabaster figure of Athena. "Remarkable. It's like a hidden treasure, right behind the gates as you drive by, and who would know. On an English country lane. It isn't in any of the tour books, is it? Bramsfield Castle? I read about this region when Aunt Evie first moved here. And then I researched it again, well, research is an over-statement, I googled it when the children were coming for summer. Things to do in Hampshire. Didn't come up."

"Yes, we like to think we're a well-kept secret," the museum guard said, looking directly at Tess when he said it.

"Some secrets are best if they're kept," he added, "don't you think, M'Lady, that's part of the fun of them. Don't you think?" He addressed this to Tess, although he turned and looked at Max, too, after he'd said it the second time, but he didn't wait for them to answer.

"There it is up ahead," he said, "the merry-go-round."

Tess wanted to run through the turnstile. She wanted to make a wish. There were the four horses. Sir Baldemare looking more noble than he ever had before and slightly mischievous, even though he was a bit dusty. She wondered, if they walked farther, if they'd find a black stallion up in the stable.

The carousel existed. Was that the sign she was looking for? That she hadn't imagined it, after all. *Was the carousel itself a sign? Or just the fact of the castle?*

Did she need a sign, at all? The museum guard had winked at her when he'd said it and then he repeated himself, "Some secrets are best kept, don't you think, M'Lady?"

"I don't know," she said. "I suppose that might be right."

Tess felt herself leaning on the turnstile, trying to resist the impulse to make a wish.

"I'm afraid it's jammed shut. It won't turn any more."

"Won't it?" said Tess as the turnstile swung around the moment she touched it with her hip—it didn't even need the push of her hand.

As she stepped in, the carousel came immediately to life, lit up in sparkles as if there were a hundred candles behind the tiny inset mirrors at the top. The music came on at full orchestral pitch, playing some kind of old-fashioned circus song. *Oom Pah Pah Oom Pah Pah Oom Pah* ... with lots of bells and horns and violins behind it— the kind of song that might have been played by a sitting orchestra in the early 1900s.

"Wow, that's impressive," said Max.

"I've never seen it happen before," the museum guard said quickly. As the lights continued to glow, the music blared, and the merry-go-round started to spin around, he added, looking at Tess, "I've heard there's an automatic switch underneath the concrete that turns it on when you step on it."

"Is there?" said Tess. "Really? I thought it was magic."

The merry-go-round slowed to a stop but the lights continued to glow, sparkling softly, the dappled gray pony stopped beside her—Sir Baldemare, her knight—as if beckoning her to get on.

"I'm sorry, M'Lady," the museum guard said before she could even make a move toward the merry-go-round. "I'm not sure the carousel is safe to ride."

Tess could've seconded that one. But out loud, she only said, "Can I ask you something? Were they ever re-united? The boy's father and mother? Did they ever find each other again?"

"That they did, M'Lady. But it took a blue moon."

Somehow, she'd expected that would be the answer.

She exited the turnstile. The merry-go-round went dark the moment she stepped outside.

She turned to her father. "I'm sorry, Daddy," she said.

"We must have the wrong house. Don't you think, Max? Surely if there'd been a carousel, someone would've shown it to us. Don't you think, Max? And a sculpture garden? And an elaborate maze?"

Max nodded back at her but didn't say a word.

"Thank you," she said to the museum guard, "for giving us a tour. I hope maybe you'll, ummm, let us come back some day."

"I would like that, M'Lady. Any time you can." Tess wasn't sure but she thought he winked slightly at her when he said this.

She took one last look at the garden: the row of hawthorn trees, she knew what was on the other side; the pond that today had both frogs and swans; the bed of white roses splendidly in bloom. She reached down to her boot, as if she had an itch, and felt the key. She heard William's voice in her head. *Keep the key,* he'd said, *you never know when you might need it.*

acknowledgments

When I was a kid, I thought of books as magical adventures, places I could get lost in, almost like an alternative universe. I believed (and still do) that the characters existed, the worlds they travelled in were real, even though they were sometimes fanciful and clearly invented. Sometimes I feel that way also when I'm writing a book, and writing this book, for me, was a magical journey. As with all journeys, it had a couple of twists and turns before it found its way (magically) inside these covers and I'd like to thank a few people who were guideposts along the way.

Maia, Anna, & Ethan, my children, who are always my inspiration, and Rachel, my step-daughter, whose love of horses and indomitable spirit also inspires; my sister Delia, whose defiant, unflagging support and extraordinary determination I carry with me every day; Jill Santopolo, my editor, who deserves more adjectives than this page allows, an amazing superb astonishing treasure who is an indulgent yet ever-so-meticulous editor who is quite simply a pleasure to work with and for, the brilliant, pitch-perfect, steady eye of publisher Michael Green, the brilliant uncanny eye of book designer Jennifer Chung, Talia Benamy, cover artist Jennifer Bricking and map artist Vartan Ter-Avanesyan, and everyone else at Philomel, whose enthusiasm, support, kindness, and love of whimsy are a delight; Nick Pileggi, Allison Thomas, and John Byers for their kind ears, humor, and advice; Kari Stuart and Amanda Urban for their watchful and careful agenting eyes; Bob Myman, my attorney, whose validation means more to me than he knows; and Alan Rader, my husband, my partner, whose support, love, and constant belief in me are a wonder to behold.

And to everyone who believes that just down the road there might be a secret door to a castle if you only knew where to find the key and that wishes, especially well thought of ones, can sometimes come true.

TURN THE PAGE
TO ENTER ANOTHER FANTASTICAL
WORLD WITH TESS AND MAX IN—

the cottage at devon-by-the-sea

I'll take the attic," said Tess, tearing up the third flight of stairs before Max even had a chance to fully understand the question.

"It's a three-bedroom house," Aunt Evie had said when they walked in the door, "four, if you count the attic. So, since your parents are coming in a few days, one of us has to take the attic... and I don't think it's going to be me."

"It's mine," said Tess emphatically. She thought an

attic bedroom was possibly a charming idea, a little scary but in a good way. It also occurred to her that her brother, Max, might be a little scared if he slept up there—even though he wouldn't want to admit it—so she instantly claimed it.

Tess hesitated on the landing at the top of the stairs. She held her breath as she popped the door open, frightened it might be dusty, musty, or dotted with spiders, but the room was flooded with sunlight from a triangular window that looked out on to the sea. It was a small room—well, tiny, but blue-and-white striped wallpaper lined two of the walls, and the wall with the window was painted white so that it was almost cheerful.

There was a double bed covered with a down quilt and big white pillows. The ceiling sloped down a bit like a triangle toward the window, so she figured she had to be careful getting out of bed on the right side.

Note to self: remember to always get up on the left side of the bed so as not to bump your head.

Tess could hear the sound of the ocean lapping softly against the shore. And even inside the air was fresh, a tiny bit salty and moist from the sea. It occurred to Tess that she was really going to like Devon-by-the-Sea on top of that strange thing that had already happened that she didn't think she could tell Aunt Evie about.

a plane, a train, a car ride, and a trip to the zoo

here's what had already happened

Their mom, Abby, had taken them to the international terminal at JFK Airport. They checked in with the help of a very nice porter who told them, after he helped carry their bags to the counter, that he hoped they had an excellent adventure.

Tess hoped they had an excellent adventure, too.

Their mother then escorted them as far as she could, to the security line.

Tess dropped her backpack. She hugged her mother and gave her a kiss on both cheeks since, after all, they were going to Europe, and kissing people on both cheeks was the custom there. Max just nodded when his mom smooshed his hair on the top of his head, which was a funny way she had sometimes of sending him off to school in the morning. But then he dropped his backpack, too, and gave her a hug and a kiss on the cheek. Then Tess and Max were on their own.

They waited patiently in line for their turn to go through the metal detector. Max went first. Then Tess.

For reasons Tess couldn't understand, when she walked through the metal detector, there was suddenly a very large noise as the alarm went off. She turned around. She was certain she couldn't have done that. But everyone at the checkpoint was looking at her. The TSA officer, who wasn't nearly as nice as the porter, directed her, as if it was a command, to walk back through the machine.

"It must be my cap," said Tess instantly, realizing she'd forgotten to take her olive-green baseball cap off. It didn't have any lettering on it at all, no advertising; it didn't draw any attention to itself, just kept the sun off, which is what Tess thought was the perfect thing for a cap. She gently placed it on the conveyor belt.

"Are *you* wearing a belt?" the TSA officer asked her.

"Nope." She shook her head. Then wondered if *nope* was the right thing to say to a TSA officer.

"Is your cell phone in your pocket?"

"No," she answered.

"Do you have any keys?" he asked her.

"Oh," she said. *She was frightened he was going to take it away from her.*

She pulled an old-fashioned skeleton key out of her front jeans pocket. "Of course! It's—the key to my aunt's house in London," she said.

This was the first lie Tess had told in a long time, but she knew she couldn't tell him what it was really. *She was frightened he might ask to see it.* It was the key to the gate at the castle next door to her aunt's house in Hampshire, the key to her friend William's garden, but that seemed way too hard to explain . . .

When Tess was packing, she'd heard William's voice so clearly, as clearly as if he was standing next to her, saying the last thing he'd said to her last summer. "Keep the key," he'd said, "you know never when you might need it."

Tess thought it was opportune of her to take the skeleton key with her to England—that was a word their Dad used, "opportune," it implied it might be useful later—and

Tess thought that might actually be the case because, in her experience, you never knew what could happen in England.

"We need it," she said to the TSA officer, her voice pitching up a little bit when she said it.

Her brother, Max, chimed in from the other side of the checkpoint, "We do. Aunt Evie said we should bring it." Max was lying, too.

The TSA officer hesitated for a moment. It felt like a long moment to Tess. "All right, then," he said, finally, without asking to see it.

She'd been so frightened he would ask to see it. She never was quite sure what the key was going to do if she handed it to someone else. She remembered what had happened when Max had found it by mistake last summer and it had turned bright red and burned his hand . . .

"Is this your backpack?" he asked. The TSA officer pointed to a kid-size version of a military-green backpack sitting alone at the end of the conveyor belt that in fact belonged to Tess. "Do you think you could put that key in your luggage, where it belongs?"

"Yes, Sir," she said. He handed it back, around the X-ray machine, and watched while she unzipped the side pocket, carefully dropped the key in, and zipped the pocket back up. She realized she'd been holding her breath. She had been so frightened that he might confiscate it, another one of those grown-up words that meant "take it away." She set the backpack on the conveyer belt and watched it slide again into the metal tunnel, where a picture could be viewed. Then she stepped back through the metal detector, and thankfully neither she or the backpack set off any further alarms.

Almost the second the plane leveled out at flying altitude, Max fell asleep.

Tess wrote a story in her notebook about a little girl who falls asleep on a train and misses her stop, rides past it, and ends up in another town—that was as far as she got and then she fell asleep, too.

Tess and Max woke up almost at the same moment, somewhere over the Atlantic.

Their mom's best friend, Franny, had packed them sandwiches from the fancy delicatessen so that they wouldn't have to eat the food on the plane, which she said was full of preservatives. Their mom had slipped in some chocolate chip cookies after Franny left. They were from the bakery on the corner but they weren't sure Franny believed in sugar, either.

Tess and Max were both surprised how quickly the

pilot announced that they were about to land at Heathrow Airport.

They put their seatbacks up and Max raised the window shade, which was especially startling as the sun was just beginning to rise. The clouds were stunningly tinged with gold, blue, red, and purple rays, like a painting, and the outline of London looked like a toy city with its pitched roofs, cobblestone streets, and church steeples covered in a cloud of mist.

• • •

Aunt Evie was waiting for them at the airport. Tess heard her voice before she saw her.

"Yoo-hoo," her voice rang out clearly through the crowd.

Aunt Evie had lightened her hair. She also had a new haircut. The front was layered a bit and fell beautifully around her face and down her shoulders, and she was wearing a bit of makeup and what looked to Tess like a *new* summer dress. Tess didn't know if her aunt was feeling "chipper," an English word for "cheerful," or if it was just the way Aunt Evie dressed to go to London, but either way Tess thought her mom would think it was a good sign:

that maybe Aunt Evie was cheering up, coming out of her shell a bit. Aunt Evie had understandably been sad since her husband, their uncle John, had died so unexpectedly in a skiing accident three winters before. She had moved to their country house in Hampshire and practically holed herself up alone for a year and a half except for the month last summer when Tess and Max visited her. Aunt Evie was only thirty-nine, which their mom said was very young to be a widow. Aunt Evie was wearing a yellow sleeveless summer dress and high-heeled sandals.

Max made her smile when he said instantly, "You look awfully pretty, Aunt Evie." It was the first they'd seen her in almost a year.

Tess and Max had spent the school year in New York City with their mom. Their dad, Martin Barnes, a well-known newscaster and sometimes war reporter, had left in February.

He'd been made the head of the news desk in Berlin, which didn't really mean he was in Berlin. Berlin was mostly used as a jumping-off spot to parts of Europe, Russia, and the Middle East, so they were never quite certain where he was and if they were supposed to be worried about him . . .

Their mom, Abby Barnes, had stayed in New York

with them so that they could finish out the school year, Max, fourth grade, and Tess, fifth. Also, their mom was a writer and she had a book due.

Their mom and dad hadn't seen each other for three months, so they were going on a grown-up mini vacation, a long weekend, to Barcelona, Spain. Their mom's plane was leaving a few hours after theirs and the plan was, their mom and dad were going to join Tess, Max, and Aunt Evie in Devon-by-the-Sea. And maybe even take a trip to Scotland.

Aunt Evie had rented out her house in Hampshire for the summer and had rented a charming beach cottage in Devon, or as she called it, "Devon-by-the-Sea," which was really just a geographical designation, but when Evie said it, it sounded as if it was a magical name.

Aunt Evie had planned and researched everything in the neighborhood. There was wi-fi in the cottage and also a big, high-definition flat-screen TV on a wall in the living room. The cottage was "turn-key furnished," which means it came with practically everything: tables, chairs, couches, sheets, towels, pots, and pans.

There was a miniature golf course nearby, a cherry festival coming up, and a world-famous zoo that was also an animal refuge, not to mention the actual beach and the sea itself and lots of other children potentially around.

Aunt Evie really wanted Tess and Max to be happy and occupied this summer. She'd even bought an iPhone herself, so that they would always be able to reach her, and she'd set up an Instagram account, even though she wasn't exactly up-to-speed on how to post on it. Her Instagram handle was @YrAuntEvie. The first photo she posted was a view out the living room window of the beach cottage in Devon-by-the-Sea, the day she rented it. The wood window frame was almost like a frame to the view in the picture. The sky was gray, the ocean was a little gray, too, with tiny white tops to the waves, and white sand, like a washed-out watercolor.

She added a caption.

Guess where I am?

Answer: Devon-by-the-Sea

Max figured it out instantly, though the location was obvious because she said that right in the caption. "Do you think she's rented a beach house?" he asked his mom, showing her the picture. Her mother knew the answer as Aunt Evie had called her to discuss the plan. "Yes, Max," she answered, "I think she has. Although she called it a turn-key cottage."

Max asked Tess if she thought there were any ghosts in

the cottage. Their mom overhead and answered instantly, "I'm not sure that's what turn-key means." But Tess and Max, who'd been on a trip to England before and had a very curious experience with a key, weren't sure that they agreed.

• • •

From Heathrow, they took a taxi to Paddington Station in London. In the back of the cab, Tess unzipped her backpack and put the skeleton key safely in her back pocket.

They boarded a train to Exeter, approximate train travel time three and a half hours, according to Max, who looked it up on his iPhone. They arrived three minutes early.

Aunt Evie had parked her blue Bentley at the train station earlier that day. It was comforting to see it there (and a little bit exciting), like running into an old friend. Tess sat in the back seat, as usual, so Max could sit in the front seat as he sometimes got carsick. Aunt Evie put the top down and tied her hair up in a ponytail.

Tess looked out the window as they drove. The landscape was so green, what their mom would call "pastoral," high grass dotted with wildflowers. They headed south on the windy highway, which curved left, then right along the countryside. Tess saw a young woman with long brown hair tied back loosely under a riding cap, riding on a spectacularly beautiful chestnut-colored horse, pedigree, for sure. The woman was wearing a fancy jacket and breeches, English riding pants, and boots that looked like they could walk on their own. But what struck Tess most was the single fluidity with which she rode, as if she really was one with the horse.

Tess had a sudden idea. She thought it would be amazing to ride a horse on the beach at night. She was careful not to wish for it. She knew from last summer that it was best to save your wishes for things that might be *really* important. But she thought she might tell her aunt about it later, just in case there might be a stable in the neighborhood where you could rent a horse for an afternoon or an evening.

The woman riding looked over at Tess for a moment and nodded and then seemed to race along with them, keeping pace with the Bentley, until a wide open field came into view and the woman guided the horse to make a right turn and then raced away, leaving a trail of brown dust in their wake before they seemed to disappear.

• • •